Studies in the Book Machine
(March 2/82)

1

(page)

TRUTH

a book of fictions

bpNichol

Edited by Irene Niechoda

THE MERCURY PRESS

ACKNOWLEDGEMENTS
The publisher gratefully acknowledges the financial assistance of the Canada Council, the Ontario Arts Council, and the Ontario Ministry of Culture through the Ontario Publishing Centre.

The publisher thanks Diane Martin, Steve McCaffery, Ellie Nichol, and Irene Niechoda.

§

Some of these fictions have appeared elsewhere in *Canadian "Pataphysics* (Underwhich, 1980), *Ink, Open Letter, Rampike, Raven, York Bulletin*, & in publications by *Letters* and *curvd H&z*. Apologies for any previous publications lost in the lacunae.

"Probable Systems 36: Digging up the Pas T" was presented at the symposium of Linguistic Onto-Genetics (Toronto, 21 November, 1981), & previously published as no. 5 of *grOnk, final series* (Toronto, 1985). "To Speak Two" is a collaboration with Lola Lemire Tostevin, & was published in her *Double Standards* (Longspoon, 1985).

Truth: A Book of Fictions is the fifth & last volume in the series initiated by *Love: A Book of Remembrances* (Talonbooks, 1972). *Zygal: A Book of Mysteries and Translations* (Coach House Press, 1985) & *Art Facts: A Book of Contexts* (Chax Press, 1990) are the second and third volumes, respectively. The fourth is *Ox, House, Camel, Door: A Book of Higher Glyphs*, publication pending.

Thanks to Diane Martin for her long-distance help.— I.N.

§

Cover design: Gordon Robertson
Cover art: bpNichol
Artwork touch-ups: Amie Daurio
Composition in Bembo and page design by TASK
Printed on acid-free paper and bound in Canada

CANADIAN CATALOGUING IN PUBLICATION:

Nichol, B. P., 1944-1988.
Truth : a book of fictions
Poems.
ISBN 0-920544-98-3
I. Niechoda, Irene. II. Title.
PS8527.I32T77 1993 C811'.54 C93-093398-2
PR9199.3.N48T77 1993

The Mercury Press is represented in Canada by the Literary Press Group, and is distributed in Canada by General Publishing and in the U.S. by Inland Book Company (selected titles).

The Mercury Press
137 Birmingham Street
Stratford, Ontario
Canada N5A 2T1

Out of kindness comes redness and out of rudeness comes rapid same question, out of an eye comes research, out of selection comes painful cattle.

— Gertrude Stein, "Tender Buttons"

Studies in the Book Machine 5
(March 3/82)

This is the
(1st) (7th)
page of the
book.

Maps

1 “a day”
a state of mind
you place yourself in

a trance
your eyes wide open or

a heightening
letting defenses drop
opening the senses
up & out
widening into the wide world

2
i don’t need the framework

i don’t need the crutch

(this is the personal section)

what i need is
the trust in
my own being

you don’t need the system

you don’t need technique
except as a way to
get you there

ready

3
the moment does not come
the moment is

continual

can you reach it

Sketch for a Botanical Drawing for Thomas A. Clark
(March 31/78)

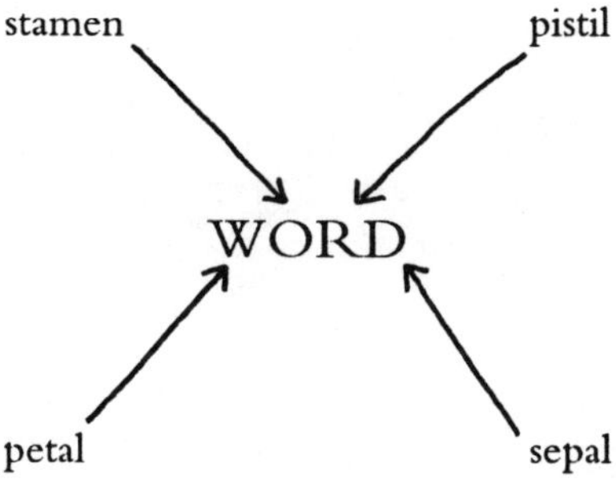

Afternoon Attentions 3

plants

p
lants

pl
ants

pla
nts

plan
ts

plant
s

plants

.

    air
  hair

chair

.

light

light light

dark light

dark dark

light dark

light light

         light

.

FIRE!

.

stick
walking
    ck
  lk
    ck
  lk
    ck

.

log

.

and a
and a
and a
and a
and a
and

Probable Systems 33: Wild Roses in Clusters

An archaelexicological excavation of issues raised by the work of Thomas A. Clark (April–May/78)

INTRODUCTION

In the last Century it was considered almost dishonest deliberately to transform a given theme into a new one, that is, to use a given theme as a basis for deducing a related theme, and there were tedious arguments about rights of existence for such derived works. Today, it is possible that every new orthodox work is only a transformation of some earlier work, made consciously or unconsciously.

So far have times changed that theme transformation has become a matter for public discussion as a meritorious proceeding. In recent times, the numerous essays to be found in journals are generally, in effect or in fact, studies in the transformation of particular themes.

No-one, however, has yet surveyed the whole field of theme transformation in detail. It is, therefore, with the belief that a real advance in the scientific understanding of relationships will be made that the present pioneer discussion has been elaborated.

I. OUTLINE OF THE PRINCIPAL METHODS OF THEME TRANSFORMATION

There are many ways of deriving a relatively new theme from an existing theme. However, they all fall into one or other of five main groups if the transformation is "primitive" in form, or into two or more of the same groups if the form is "compound."

A LINEAR TRANSFORMATION of the thought, consisting in the linear transformation of one or more of the theme elements.

B MODAL (OR ANGULAR) TRANSFORMATION in which the original line is rotated. The thematic play remains identical in principle, however.

C TRANSFORMATION OF MEDIUM (Dedicated to Falindgren on his 40th birthday)

D TRANSFORMATION OF MOTIVE where the line is geometrically identical but the motive changes.

E TRANSFORMATION BY EXTENSION (or GENERALIZATION), where the line & the themes shrink or expand.

The various subdivisions of the above general methods are discussed in subsequent sections of this essay.

Preparatory to such discussion, it will be convenient to select names for the different sorts of transformation. It has been suggested that the aggregate of linear transformations of a theme should be called the "locus" of the theme, and the individual cases "spots" on the locus. But the latter word is really intolerable for serious usage, and I propose the following system of terminology:

TRANSFORMATIONS	NAMES FOR INDIVIDUAL EXAMPLES
1. Linear	Aspects
2. Modal (Angular)	Modes
3. Medium	Types
4. Motive	Forms
5. Generalization	Generalization

"Mode" is now commonly used in method 2 and "Form" is forced upon us by the antiform transformation which is an outstanding sub-division of method 4. The other words will probably prove acceptable for general use, e.g. "type" adapts itself readily to B-type, R-type, and similar combinations needed in discussing the medium of representation of a theme. "Aspects" at any rate retains four letters of the stupid "spots"! It reads smoothly in such phrases as— Nos. 1 and 2 are different aspects of the theme.

It will soon be realized as we proceed that the exigencies of practical construction make it rarely possible to apply only one of these methods of transformation, and that the majority of examples superpose several of them. For clarity of discussion, however, it is often necessary to particularize only one change for the time being. As the argument expands, further reference will be made to other features of such compound transformations.

II. LINEAR TRANSFORMATION

Linear transformation consists, in formal language, in the translation of one or more theme elements relative to the rest. In its pure, or better "primitive," form, it will involve no change in the angles, medium, motive, or extent of the theme, but such absolute purity of change is rare. Inevitably there is often considerable alteration in the non-thematic constituents, and just where these cease to be part of the theme is a matter of arbitrary choice. Themes may be described also with various degrees of generality and the nature of a transformation may be affected considerably by such narrowing or broadening of the thought.

Another element of every theme is the page itself, and linear displacement in relation to the page edges in some cases has striking results. But most themes are little affected by sliding along the page.

It may be noted that in general the Writer derives much more satisfaction from linear transformation than does the Reader. To the latter, the different aspects of a theme may not appear to vary very much and he may not escape a sense of monotony. The Writer, however, finds in general that the constructive details vary in endless subtle ways, while some aspects obstinately defy representation, so that he recaptures in full the spirit of creative struggle, success in which is the only reward worthwhile in such work.

III. MODAL (ANGULAR) TRANSFORMATION

The modal method of transforming themes consists in altering the angles between two or more linear theme elements. It is therefore seen to the best advantage in multi-line themes, though as will appear later line-play is not an essential for modal transformation.

In general in any theme with two or more lines, the angles between these lines may be changed in obvious ways. Unlike the linear method, these modal alterations lead to sharply distinctive texts quite devoid of monotony for the reader.

The angular (and in part, linear) changes in the lines are often manifest in the shapes of the basic triangle. But there is a more subtle angular transformation possible, the rotation of a theme line through 180 degrees, in other words, the line considered as to its direction usually runs from left to right but when transformed runs from right to left, a rotation of 180 degrees. It is plainly possible, as well, to put words BETWEEN the key words in such cases.

As in the case of linear transformation, an important type of modal transformation consists in altering the angle of the whole theme relative to the poem's visual lines. It is in this form that the subject is best known. In Found Poetry this subtype receives an infinity of new angles for application. One phase of modal transformation relative to the page that may be overlooked, however, is that of themes rotated through 180 degrees or 90 degrees. These changes do not alter the theme relative to the orthogonal lattice itself, but they do alter it relative to the page considered as a directed space in virtue of the words "top" and "bottom" at its ends. Generally speaking these changes may vitally affect the writer— witness his free use of "turning the page" to overcome constructive difficulties— but they have relatively minor effects on the theme per se, and the reader will usually overlook their existence.

A particular case of modal change relative to the page is that of reflection. If the reflection is in any axis other than a vertical one, the result in general will be identical with the rotation just discussed. Further, pure reflection of any THEME in a vertical axis will have no effect on it whatever.

Hitherto the modal changes considered have related almost exclusively to alterations in the angles of particular or individual lines. Modal change may be applied, however, to whole groups of lines and consequently to whole groups of points where no lines occur at all. An echo may reveal itself in such a linear translation, or in some angular motion (rotation or reflection) or, of course, in a combination of motions. There is no need to give illustrations of this well-known subject, but it may not be realized that the same kind of transformation— by echo— may be applied, on a still larger scale as it were, in two or more texts, the TEXTS (or their themes) being echoes of one another.

The ways in which a text may repeat a thought with some modal variation are not, certainly, endless, but it is difficult to see the end.

IV. TRANSFORMATION OF MEDIUM

The poetic medium comprises space, words, and limitations. Transformation of any of these elements may have all degrees of effect, from scarcely perceptible to very remarkable, on theme type.

The casual change of parts of speech in a theme, although one of the commonest devices, is on the whole not a very successful operation in normal poetry. There are, however, three outstanding cases where the method creates excellent effects.

The first of these is the geometrical procedure of altering parts of speech in relation to modal transformations, which has very successful results. The stress here, however, is on angular changes rather than on changes in words needed to supply the angles.

The second case is the group of themes connected with the maximum number of meanings capable of being delivered by each word or specific combination of words.

The third case is that of transforming themes by giving a key word one or more parts of speech it can move through at random, which is tantamount to using a new type of word, and which is very successful in modifying many themes.

Change of limitations is a subject specific to Found Poetry, and an infinitely rich one. Its study leads to the empirical discovery, obvious enough when made, that particular systems of limitations are extraordinarily adaptable to some themes and highly improper for others. The normal limitations share this property, being extremely useful in some directions and the very reverse in others.

There is no need to give numerous examples of change of limitation here, since the basic theme or thought is displayed in terms of different Found Poetry types, with results often more characteristic of the type than of the theme.

V. TRANSFORMATION OF MOTIVE

The outstanding case of transformation of motive is that from Primitive to Antiform theme. The subject has been adequately discussed in a number of essays, pamphlets and books, but it should be noticed that three thematic elements are involved SIMULTANEOUSLY in the Antiform transformation. They are:

1 The Primitive or Antiform mechanism of the theme.
2 Involvement in the inclusion of words or exclusion of words by the writer (or the reader).
3 Involvement Directly, of free will, or Indirectly, under compulsion.

These three elements are bound together by a relationship of invariant character which can be put in mathematical terms, as I showed in the Hamburgischer Correspondent, 6/7/1924:

Thus, if F denotes the "form" (element 1 above) and the signs plus (+) and minus (-) are assigned arbitrarily to the two forms; and if Wr denotes the writer/reader (element 2 above) and the signs plus and minus are assigned arbitrarily to the inclusion & exclusion of words; and if V denotes the volition (element 3 above) and the signs plus and minus are assigned arbitrarily to direct and indirect involvement; then whichever sign the product FWrV assumes in any one text illustrating a given theme in a given medium, FWrV will remain CONSTANT to that sign for EVERY TRANSFORMATION, of the antiform kind, of that theme in that medium.

It follows that every such transformation involves the inversion of TWO elements and two only, inversions of one or three elements simultaneously being impossible, a rather striking restriction.

The reason for this law is quite simple. It is found in the easily established fact that the inversion of any single element transforms an "advantageous" sequence into a "disadvantageous" one for a given writer/reader. But in texts all in one medium and theme all the texts must require the same kind of "advantageous" aim to come to a successful conclusion, so that single changes are impossible, and two have to be made to change the "advantage" into another "advantage."

The possibility of transforming a single element arises only by changing the aim of the combination, what would be a "meaningful" involvement having to become a "meaningless" one, or vice versa.

Changes in the motives governing the meaning of individual words— they may well be called Tactical Transformations— are another very common feature. They tend to produce quite distinctive thematic forms and provide the writer with enjoyable specific difficulties.

The transformations of motive affects the principal idea of the text, but transformations of some quite minor or subtle detail of motive in a text may be equally effective in developing widely differing forms.

VI. TRANSFORMATION BY EXTENSION OR GENERALIZATION

The extension of a given theme may proceed along one or other of three lines, all closely associated since extension is always extension, but sufficiently distinctive to be considered apart. They are the lines of extension of mechanism, of cumulative multiplication of the given thought, and of generalization in its true connotation.

One very simple but excellent device for complicating many themes, and usually calling for considerable extension of the machinery, is to assign a word one or more parts of speech. This process has already been referred to in Section 4 as tantamount to using a new kind of word.

The extension of a given theme on the cumulative principle, multiplying elements already present, may proceed on either of two slightly dissimilar paths. We may extend the one theme, obtaining more elements in a unified scheme, or we may multiply the number of themes either by repetition or addition of new themes. But this last idea in Found Poetry is very much weakened by the simple fact that any theme we care to select can always be multiplied to infinity— using the word "infinity" in its correct connotation— so that there is some lack of enthusiasm for merely finite results.

It is perhaps a suitable moment to note that the great majority of transformations discussed in this essay contain no example. This choice was deliberate, to make the thematic transformations conspicuous and as easily understood as possible. It is perhaps scarcely necessary to add that there is nothing in the nature of the methods discussed which forbids their application to themes of any length or order of complexity.

Excavated from T.R. Dawson's *Five Classics of Fairy Chess* (Dover, 1973).

Craft Dinner

blue blue blue. brown & green. bluer & bluer. i thot i blew her up like a balloon. was it fun? she seemed too flighty to me i couldn't tie her down. he leapt out of the pages at me. i closed the book. grey. blue grey blue. blue in blue surrounded by blue with another blue emerging. hello & goodbye. not again! only blue. bluest of blues. blue.

red. yellow. blue. red yellow blue. redyellowblue! green. un- no.
blue red yellow. green. yellow red. red. blue yellowbluered! yes.
un- no. un-a- yes. un- no no. -a-
                                                            that. this or that. this
but that. or. but also. and &. but. or this. or that. or this or
that. also.
                        bled. rue. bledrue. no. bled but. yes. ruebled.
yes. rubble. yes.
                                un- un-un-a- un-a-bled-abled-rue
                                                                                that. this
also. this. or that this. unabluerue red. bled.
                                                                        green. or yellow.
yellow green yellows red. this
                                            living
                                        particular conscious mental acts
                                        immediate
                                        plot
                                        blue
                                        where
                                        idea of
                                        distortion
                                        interesting
                                        almost automatic
                                                                a continuation. something
like speech likes. lately. up. down &. down & up. stop.
                                                                                    green. &
something
                        or something else
both ways a middle beginning ending

The Elevation of Saint Ranglehold

```
         8888888888888888888888888888888888
         8888888888888888888888888888888888
         88888888                888      888
         88888888      oo        888      888
         88888888      oo        888      888
         88888888                888      888
         8888888888888888888888888888888888
         8888888888888888888888888888888888
                               999
                               999
                               999
                               999
                               999
                               999
                               666
                               666
                               666
                               666
                               666
                               666
888888888888888888888888888888888888888888888
888888888888888888888888888888888888888888888
888888888                      888       8888
888888888                      888  ...  8888
888888888                      888  ...  8888
888888888                      888       8888
888888888888888888888888888888888888888888888
```

4 Moods
(1986/87)

1) The Friendliness of the Alphabet

abcdefgHIjklmnopqrstuvwxyz

2) The Denial of the Alphabet

abcdefghijklmNOpqrstuvwxyz

3)The Sanctimoniousness of the Alphabet

abcdefghijklmnopqrSTuvwxyz

4)The Self-Centredness of the Alphabet

abcdefghIjklmnopqrstuvwxyz

Studies in the Book Machine 1: A Sketch
(March 2/82)

TWO

PAGES

Dequence

vote
devote
sire
desire
scant
descant

Robotics
(January 24/79)

1

mechanization
(futurist dreams)

the fascism of
the microphone
not to be confused with
technology per se
(pen, paper, etc.)

sex confused with
machine function
(we have no
feelings, etc.)

machine $\neq$ unconscious
machine = abandoned consciousness
(careless driving, etc.)

you get arrested

2

forward motion
backward motion
emotion

consequences of
current feelings

electric in the chair

how do you get there?

dead ahead
the switch

gearing up
you could go either way

fearing or
hearing

3

lost in flesh

id ideas

the notion is
increased motion

speed

you break the sound barrier
get further & farther away from
your own words

you can't break the light barrier

the sight travels with you

tough memories

4

l e
le elevator

ho ho tel

T.V.
tell no vision

video image
surrounded by
the lights of
Toronto
(i.e. the old poetic image
—we define the place by
electricity)

plastic pen

felt tip technology
at my finger slips

5

four hundred & one cars go by
five hours to
dawn

measuring as if that had significance

dada dreams
mama chines

baba
to the sheep of
this life

everything disintegrates
even as the eye
beholds it

we can't unwrap the present

a bow to the bow
ties me to this moment
um
er

hrumpph

(human failure, etc.

let's avoid the tying off of
the process)

—clump—

(one shoe)

____
____
____
still waiting

(May 25/73)

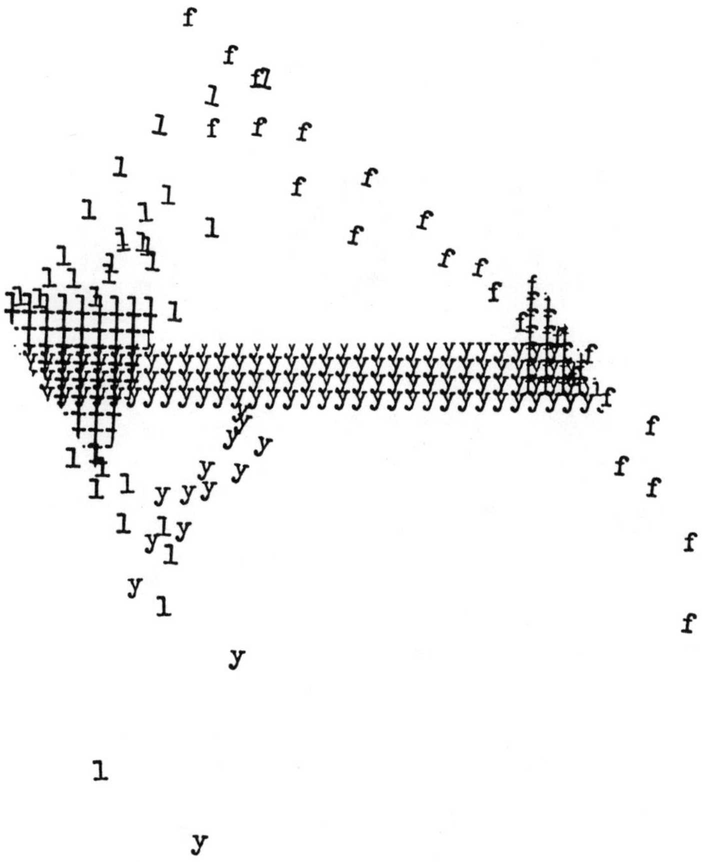

Studies in the Book Machine 2
(March 2/82)

N

I

N

E

P

A

G

E

S

Winter: 35th Year

i have travelled longer on this road than i thot i would

the mountains & the oceans lie far behind me
as far as the bed where my mother & my father dream

& i have come across the flat lands thru the forests
talking with friends about the difficulties of the journey

it is night now

midway between this world & another
the feet step from daylight into darkness

here we are all growing older
wiser perhaps
at least more confused

but there is the love
something we have worked at

a bottle of wine shared with a friend &

the songs Lord
so glad to still be singing these songs

Late Night Autumn Poem
(October 24/78)

flyth
nightnd
mmmmmmmmmmm

O

bird

bird

bird

The Ascension of William Blake

SANS SERIF–NOVELTY

Radiant Medium ABCDEF
Radiant Medium: 12 14 18 24 30 36 42 48 60 72

Radiant Bold Extra Condensed ABCDEF
Radiant Bold Extra Condensed: 14 18 24 30 36 42 48

Radiant Bold Condensed ABCDE
Radiant Bold Condensed: 12 14 18 24 30 36 42 48 60 7

Radiant Bold ABCDEFG
Radiant Bold: 12 14 18 24 30 36 42 48 60 72

Radiant Heavy ABCDEF
Radiant Heavy: 12 14 18 24 30 36 42 48 60 72

Point to Point: In an Imagined H
(Rivoli Poetry Sweatshop, February 18/87)

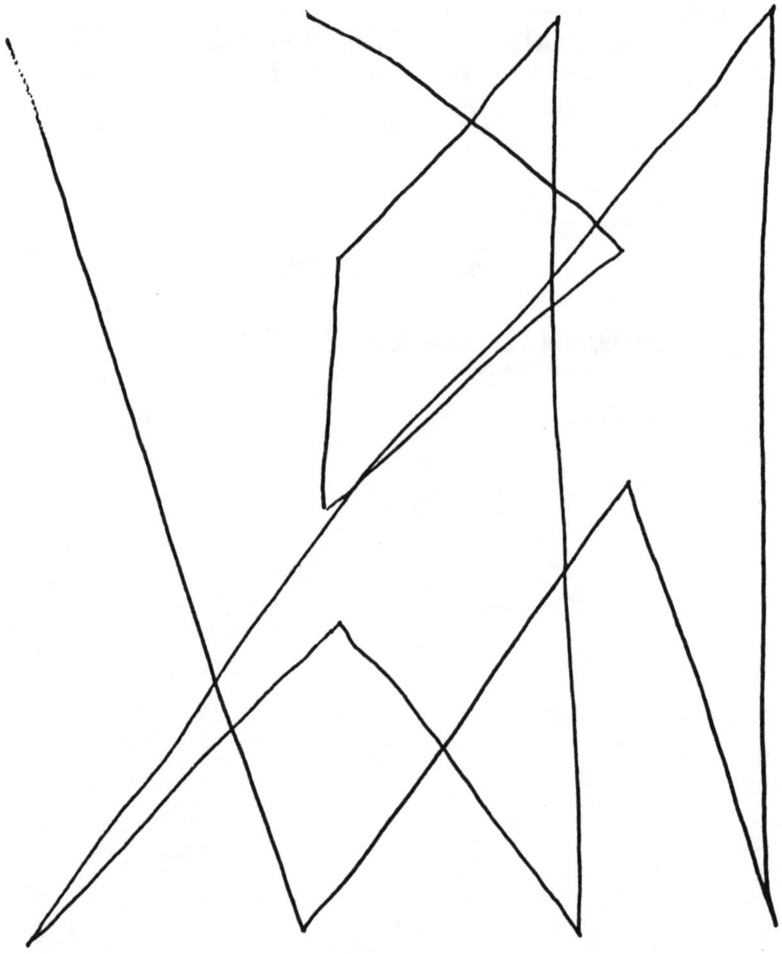

Probable Systems 14: Re-discovery of the 22 Letter Alphabet: An Archaeological Report

(1972)

what follows grows out of probable systems 11   out of W· the ear hears the UU connection   we could read the ending of the alphabet then UVUUXYZ   thus the question becomes why the double u   is it necessary

connect back to *aitch* (H) the other letter whose name falls outside the normal pattern of alphabetic naming   what seems obvious is that both letters are palindromes   AHIMOTUVWX & sometimes Y (possible connection to the real vowels of the language?) are all palindromes   in French W pronounces as double V   X is also double v   X as a human sign balances   it has the head & the genitals   W brings everything up into the head   it doubles the head's power by sacrificing the genitals

O is more than a palindrome   it reads the same from any positioning   a 25 letter alphabet allows one to return O to a centrality between m & n

M & N   here the upper case conceals   m + n contain a counter aspect and aspect of compression   2 into 1   it seems possible that n could have preceded m following the 1 to 2 numerical progression   emphasis on the 2 (m being placed first) reinforces the W preceding X (head dominated) dictum

M is the mirror image of W   narcissus   the head falls in love with the head   W is an acting out of the narcissistic fantasy   thus

X is closer to O than any other letter   both are more than palindromic   they are conjoined things & not split   T functions as a truncated I & thus the lower case t Christ's crucified on (cf. i   the ascendancy of the dot from the confining line into infinite space)   A V connect   A arising out of the OX's head note the OX connection making the A V connection clear

vis-à-vis Alfred Kallir

here the line in A actually functions as the head's top   thus in V the mind is blown   the top lifted the soul drifts free into the cosmos

V W X falsely places western intellectualization (the W as dominant head control) ahead of the X (marks the spot   the buried treasure   that which is under i.e. genital)

U V X Y Z

thus a 23 letter alphabet records a progression from earth bound A to cosmos bound V leading into ultimate freedom & connected being X (the unknown factor) it is Y Z makes X unknown they are perhaps later historically a later unlearning of the A to X tradition because X is so obviously a terminal point (marks the spot where the digging should begin   the connected self)   Y Z prevents the true functioning of X

palin-dromic letters mark key points necessary for the understanding the alphabet (alpha's bet   A's gamble   cf. PILGRIM'S PROGRESS etc.)   H & I have the most perfect relationship being palindromic, mirror reversible & reflective as well as lying next to each other in the alphabet   one rotates into the other   aitch is I's magic name   thus to know aitch is to control I   the knowledge of I (self) is impossible without the knowledge of H (I's real name)   in the 23 letter alphabet the I to N passage makes plain what the I to M passage in the 26 character one confuses   in the former m becomes the spiritual twinning of the self presaging the X conclusion   in the latter M becomes the western intellectualization of the (earlier) eastern experience

note that the secret doctrine of M & N exists in the lower case   it is placement determines misconception here   M W reads as one of the most powerful palindromic mirror-reflective units in the alphabet if its secret doctrine is understood French gives us a clue   W is double V   thus the X connective & the realization of W for what it is   if however M is understood as m & W as uu the connective doctrine emerges from the 23 letter alphabet because n & u's mirror-reversed & reflected image   thus A's gamble pays off in the movement from n thru o to m then on into t (as we've seen) u v x   thus the restoration of the real alphabet (the realphabet) becomes central to 20th century concerns of death reversal

A B C D E F G H I J K L N O M P Q R S T U V X

here it is necessary to go into the b p q d relation which emerges in the lower case secret doctrine   note that p q lie next to one another in the alphabet thus repeating the H I phenomenon   echoing as it does the b d relationship (it is its mirror-reflective image) it reveals in cluster a zygal configuration

bd
pq

thus the movement from b to q is a journey thru the zygal maze suggesting another point of restructure besides the historical necessity of the b c d cluster (see the Coda to *The Martyrology* Book III) the realization of C as a part of O structure reveals its twin in U of the central O further suggesting that U upper case was once Ɔ & that only the lower case was u (lower case completing & tying in the n) further a re-positioning of p q & U is pointed to in order to complete the palindromic elements leading us to

ABCDEFGHIJKLNOMRSTPƆQVX

thus in a certain sense the movements from A to V are contained in parentheses however in our current structuring b & q lie outside them suggesting a further re-structuring

ACBDEFGHIJKLNOMRSTPQƆVX

considered then as a complete unit the SECRET NARRATIVE of the alphabet becomes

A(BDEFGHIJKLNOMRSTPQ)V=X

thus

(A↔V)=X

X is the transformational symbol for the alphabet (note that the C Ɔ configuration is retained suggesting the whole could be written

$$\textcircled{A\leftrightarrow V} = X$$

& thus the OX leading us back into A)

this leads me to believe that in the realphabet n was written ∩ thus completing the triad ∩cu (lower case) the holy trinity? having to move into upper case to complete the palindromic quartet with the Ↄ thus two more zygal configurations emerge

these are obviously the concealed transitional figures that lead from H to X formed as they are out of the elements of O they point the way to another concealed figure the magic square formed by the H I overlay

the relationship of this to the O X overlay is unmistakable

(note in both cases the sectioning of the perfect palindromic unit into 4 linking it to the C U Ↄ ∩ & b d p q units both of which are elements of zygal configurations note the linking of quartets with triadic structures)

□'s (pronounced HI) relationship to O suggests another palindromic positioning with the HI unit counting as one letter in our balancing X is actually a transformational sign for the entire alphabet (the sign of its equivalence being understood) & the actual formula for the original transformational alphabet being written (A↔V)X we leave X out in figuring the palindromic balancing point for O counting 8 positions back from the V the restructured alphabet now looks like this

ACBDEFG□JKLRNOMSTPQↃVX

however the L to l transformation in the switch to lower case & its re-inforcement of the unity principle embodied in n O etc. thru the l reading out as "one" suggests its position in front of the n as the correct one the question then becomes the position the R should be placed in lower case r suggests a transitional character between n & v which would place it in between them in our reading

ACBDEFG□JKLNOMSRTPQↃVX

T however now appears out of place note the similarity between T I & J this in itself gives us a clue to its positioning but once again it is the lower case secret doctrine (n.b. "lower" case the case beneath the one under reference back to the genital here you can see how the Y functions as a closed X actually warning us that something has been tampered with the real meaning is "closed" to us unless we re-order & thus "open up" the alphabet) gives us the solution to our problem + is the cross we have removed from the □ sign by isolating our suffering we are cut off from deeper meaning (i solating sol as sun solus as alone sol as us (seul from the French alone)) we make the false i our sun (the centre of our uni verse) thus the SECRET NARRATIVE places the T before the □ because it is an element of the developing consciousness a stage BEFORE HIgher consciousness similarly j functions as a deeper (emotionally) i, its roots below the line (rooted in the earth—in things under) thus we could write our equation

$$+ + j = \square$$

suggesting the positioning of these three characters in the realphabet should read

T J □

thus at this stage our alphabet reads

A C B D E F G T J □ K L N O Λ\ S R P Q Ɔ V X

this leaves E F G K & S both G & K are concealed zygal characters in both cases this is only revealed thru using particular visual equivalents the lower case G that is written g immediately suggests a

formation which joins together thusly

this is hinted at in the G Q g q relationship the particular cluster revealed here is of course the altered zygal formation

by compressing the figure · even further we create the magic square structure

which is obviously transitional between □ & O G then should be placed between them in the realphabet

A C B D E F T J □ K G L N O /\\ S R P Q Ɔ V X

K's position is correct because it points back to the concealed zygal formation in T + J this is revealed when K is written ƐC (obviously zygal) the revised equation then reads

(+j>□<K)

E & F are obviously altered elements of the palindrome E Ǝ which should function as parentheses for the TJ □ K equation since joined EƎ they form an upper case I (i am indebted to david aylward's ACROSTICS for this particular insight) why the Ǝ was reversed & a line dropped to make it read F can only be guessed at our realphabet now reads

A C B D E T J □ K Ǝ G L N O /\\ S R P Q Ɔ V X

note that □ has once again been restored to the 8th position forming its balance with the O note further the similarity between 8 & g (see my "The End of the Affair" in *How Do I Love Thee* for a further exploration of this)

S is simply § suggesting that m was originally written ∩∪ its positioning is correct revealing as it does the four elements of O that will recur in the secret narrative thru the equative unit ∩∪S this completes the re-structuring of the 22 letter realphabet & the consequent revelation of its secret narrative

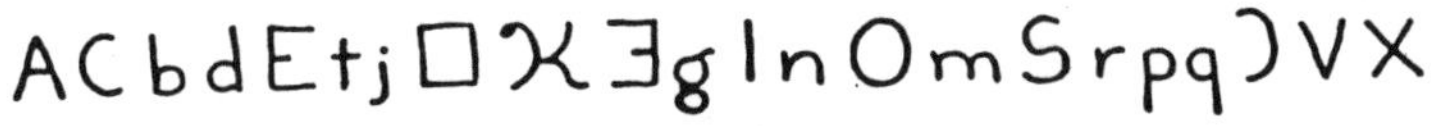

obviously W is an ambiguous letter suggesting as it does two readings the one destructive the other positive this suggests to me that it is the transitional member of the movement from X into the present Y Z terminator & is essential for a true reading of the alphabet though not of the realphabet

it should be further noted that the removal of O from its centrality in order to balance it with the HI sign is necessitated by the revelation of actual balance points in the realphabet being located in key palindromic placements & that the true secret narrative is much more complex than a simple central focal point

Kite 1
(October/71)

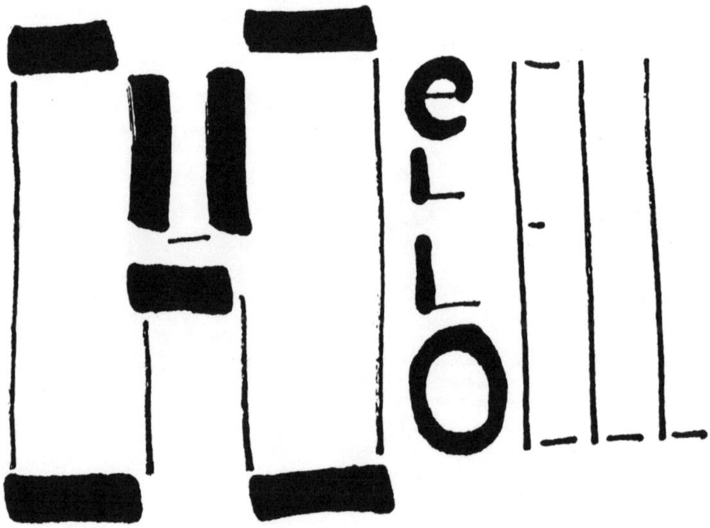

26 Crosses for the Death of Speech
(1972)

```
t     t     t     t
t     t     t     t
tora  tora  tora  tora
t     t     t     t
t     t     t     t
toronto     toronto
t                 t
```

After Words

For Gerry Gilbert

(December 2/69)

this is a poem

no it's not

nothing is ever as never was

the trees are covered in snow

a horrible day said ellie

no i said

gerry took a picture thru the window

i was sick in bed with the flu

i'm taking pictures thru everybody's window he said

hold this i didn't say handing him nothing

the sky was grey

the trees
were covered in
crumbling white leaves

Studies in the Book Machine 4
(March 2/82)

p)A(ge

To Speak Two
(Toronto, November/83 to September/84)

Each voice might appear authentic if we heard it in isolation: together, each stamps the other's with the sign of borrowing (if not of theft). — Tzvetan Todorov

your word to my sensation
your sentence in a sense
in which it can be placed
to mine
            which is the same
in which it can be named
or understood

your word
against mine

will you take my word
for it
            that particular
forêt
            les arbres
as arbitrary as
definite choice
                        les mots
("teef," he said
not having any)

turning a new leaf

to page you

"my word but
that's a nice sensation"

page me

                    is to call by name
and being called
to hear

the turning of new leaves
their falling
                              out of line

the taking of your word
your vow a vowel broken
to my silence
speaks

noun

              then

I books my's time
resisting closure

is it simply what the verb owes
gets you to
all dis continuous action

as good as your word
if you keep your word

good

·

if I keep it at all

je ne peux tenir ma parole
puisque je te l'ai donnée
parole donnée

there is no other

than coming to our terms
no other choice
this coincidence of voice
which reads between
each other's lines
each other's isolation
iso as in same
but in a different vein
the close sureness
of an ending
the entertainment of
some fiction   the crux
nailed to the page

the real friction
which is the you/I/other
ness
          open

to say for all
all that remains

the refrained refrain

part art
particular

is this

this
one
interval

Un petit poème pour Raoul

O		X
O	iseau	X
O		X

Two Blank Pages

Studies in Contradictory Information

(January 18/83)

Studies in the Book Machine 13
(January 18/83)

Other than these words the information on this page is show thru.

Homage à Mort Walker

Purge Me with H
(in progress, April 6/88)

about to kiss your h
all be as h as kings
amber scent...her h
among the heath and h's
and it shall go h
and the pursuit of h
and then take h's
angry and poor and h
as an old Parliamentary h
ask yourself whether you are h
as scant as h in leprosy
as thou woldest finde an h

bear thee up in their h's
before rude h's have touched it
better h to worse
bite the h that fed them
black, and midnight h's
boring about somebody else's h
borne a yet h thing
bracelet of bright h
braided her yellow h
bring down my grey h's
by flying h and fluttering hem
by foreign h's thy dying eyes

called "the h of men"
call no man h
case when there's h
caught the world's great h's
changed places; and h-d
Christ and all his h's
cloud like a man's h
come and cut the h
come knit h's
comes sooner by white h's
compared to h
consume h without producing it
could see to H Marshes
cursed be the h

dearer h
distinguish, and divide a h
do not h me
draw you...with a single h
drenches his h like towels
drew her long black h out
drop they "H's"
duty of being h
dying, bless the h

each particular h to stand
evening star, Love's h
every h of the bear reproduced
every h was a virgin once
everything h about him
everything h's as it should

falls not h, or rain
fasten their h's upon their hearts
fictions only and false h
find out h or not at all
finished to the last h
firmament sheweth his h
flail of the lashing h
flashing eyes, his floating h!
flies no sharp and sided h
forefathers of the h
fortress, and a dubious h

gae h, my mither dear
go into his h and pierce it
going to h him *anyhow*
great is the h that holds dominion
greatest h for the greatest numbers
greatest h of the greatest number

h: a good bank account
h a man first
h and farewell
h and marriage go by Destiny
h and wiving goes by Destiny
h -b as a picnic egg
h came, hop, hop, hop
h could I be with either
h for h, foot for foot
"h! h!" quoth he
h h h
h, h, h to my ain countree
h has become very white
h has threads of grey
h if I could say how much
h if ye seek no happier state
h in h, on the edge of the sand
h in three hundred pounds
h is crisp and even curls
h is ever at his lips
h is no laughing matter
h is not able to taste
h is too good for him
h is unworthy your acceptance
h, like thy veins
h limped trembling
h of little employment
h of my flesh stood up
h of the common man
h! our being's end
h prevents a bad marriage
"h" replied the Dodger
h's are the h's of Esau
h's brood around you
h's brown and dim-discovered spires
h's cry from street to street
h's grow hoary

h's in the hanged man's house
h sits snug in leaves
h's of your head are all numbered
h's outstretched in yearning
H's ride no more
h's that the rod of empire
h's were never made to tear
h's than I know
h that made us is divine
h that rocks the cradle
h that signed the treaty
h, the head, and the heart
h the man, and h he alone
h the man who, far from business
h themselves in hop
H, the Prince, being left out
h the test of truth
h to catch and conquer
h to execute
h too swiftly flies
h toward my hand
H Town's in Brunswick
H...village atheist
h was not told me
h was yellow like ripe corn
h women, like the h nations
h you cannot see

hat was in his h
hath not a Jew h's
hath shook h's with time
her h on her bosom
her prentice h she tried on man
here's my h
he who has once been h
hidden h is at its old game
his h's were white like wool

his h will be against every man
his red right h
hold your h but as long as all man
honour peereth in the meanest h
how h is he born
how ill white h's become
how long h ye

I am not Prince H
I do prove her h
I dwelt in marble h's
I fear thy skinny h!
if you want to win her h
I like the hunting of the h
I'll go h with him
in foul sluttish h's
in h among ladies
in nothing else so h
in the h man's house
into thy h's I commend

keep my h from picking
keep the lifted h in awe
kiss me, H

laid our groping h away
lays his icy h on kings
lend thy guiding h
let not man have the upper h
let not thy left h know
letters in a big round h
lifetime of h...hell on earth
lift my h, and eyes
lift not thy h to *It*
lifting distressful h
lion than to start a h
local h and a name
long h is a glory
long h slowly twining
look into h through another
lost our little H
Love, we are in God's h

makes the h she does not find
March H went on
merry Spring-time's h
mischief still for idle h
misery is to have been h
moral pocket h
morning star, day's h
mother bids me bind my h
my fell of h
my h is grey
my other h's are good
my own fair h

never h...but when he is drunk
no h-and-h affair
no h within this circle of flesh
no little h to wipe his little nose
no lot...h
not h for stealing horses
nothing...by which so much h
not incurious in God's h

only one thing to make me h
oozing out at the palms of my h
over in my gray h's

pale h I loved
parting line on a head of black h
perfectly h till all are h
pleasant mazes of her h
polished up that h so successfullee
pronounced on the rest of his h

rather less than h o' that
recall...h when in misery
result h
right h forget her cunning

sacred h dissever
saw H prince of Denmark
saw the air with your h
serve to pin up one's h
shake h forever
she would h on him
sight of them is necessary to h
signed it wi' his h
spirit-small h propping it
something in them to h him
some village H
subtle wreath of h
suffered many h's
sweeten this little h

take his h away
taking me up in his right h
taste not; h not
that ever wore grey h's
that would make your h curl
their h's are blue
there's a h
they gied him my h
this h hath offended
thou must bring her h
tie up my bonny brown h
to be h in a fortnight
to make men h
train of thy amber-dropping h

use doth breed a h
unless God send his h

vastly h of death
violent h's upon themselves

washed his h before the multitude
waved her lily h
wear your h like a man
we must all h together
were h and glove
we will h you, never fear
what coarse h he has!
whatsoever thy h findeth to do
when h gods go
where the kneeling h drains
who so h, — O who
will not h myself today
will these h's ne'er be clean?
with cold immortal h
with large and sinewy h
with these h's hands
won't be h till he gets it
wot's the good of H?

I.T.A.N.U.T.S. 16
(December/72)

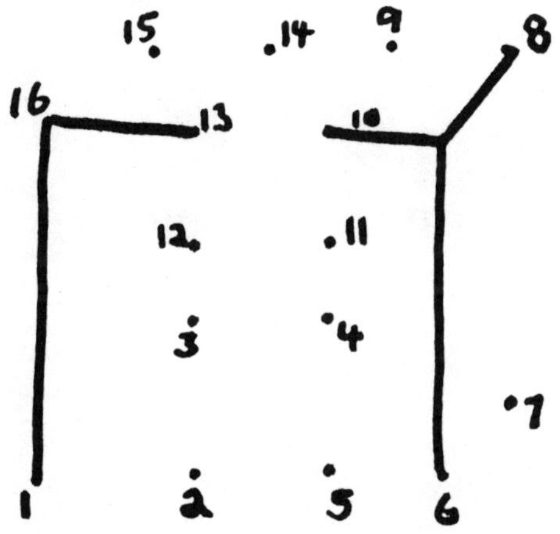

Studies in the Book Machine 9
(October 1/82)

DIRECTIONAL
BIAS

Probable Systems 36: Digging up the Pas T
(Toronto, Autumn/81)

In February 1978, during a field trip to Winnipeg, Manitoba, I discovered traces of a prehistoric alphabet cult in the form of large earthworks similar to the one at Southwold, Ontario. My first encounter with these was in the form of a map handed to me by a follower of the Ra Ma Da cult, a map charting the energy accelerators & decelerators (similar in function & concept to ley lines) that both surround Winnipeg & form a ritual routing thru the alphabetic chain.[1] Followers of Ra Ma Da had gone to great trouble & expense to sketch & print this information which, in the sea of archaeological tels that greet the concerned researcher (lumped together under the general study of Mo) has been largely overshadowed. I sketched the relevant information & new insights I was able to gain from this map in my own Probable System 18 as part of my ongoing exploration of pure language phenomena. Then in the fall of 1981 I had occasion to turn my attention to other maps of Manitoba in an attempt to uncover further traces of this same prehistoric alphabet cult the Ra Ma Da followers had so diligently recorded.

In Probable System 14 I wrote out the thinking behind my notion of the realphabet, a 22 letter system. While researching PS 18 I realized that, as in PS 14, I was dealing with concealed meanings, secret traditions that lay behind the one more commonly known. In PS 18 it took the form of partially destroyed letters & the network of accelerating & decelerating concepts I associated with the worship of the great goddess Wo.[2] Further studies, documented in PS 34, tracked the movement of gigantic airborne H's & L's over continental North America & the surrounding oceans.[3] These airborne forms, as well as the already referred to accelerators & decelerators, &, indeed, the giant letter form sites (linked to Wo but not proven) that seem to surround Winnipeg, point to alphabet worship as tied to real phenomena in the atmosphere, a time when the letter (& hence the word) was present in the world as thing, as visible fact in the land & air scapes. I had begun to suspect, further, that the alphabet cult, tho its beginnings were shrouded in pre-history, had continued in an unbroken tradition into, at least, the recent historical past, & that clues to it, & perhaps even the cult itself, must exist in the present.

Professor Michael Dean, in his ground-breaking essay "An Approach to Linguistic Onto-Genetics" (included in *Canadian "Pataphysics*) writes the telling sentence: "Language should be *the visible energy of Human Communication.*" Dean, tho he grasps the physical reality of language, & even, in his Second Law of Language, acknowledges that it "involves *Translation—transliteration and the transposition of Energy*" (in his case involving the discovery of a site now visible only as a bridge over the Amstel River), fails, in his conclusion, to make the leap of awareness that would've led him to the alphabet cult, focussing, instead, on language's acknowledged use in Human Communication & his concerns for it.

R. Truhlar, in his article "Toward A Constructivist Theory of Linguistic Onto-Genetics" (*Open Letter*, 4th ser. 6/7 [Winter 1980–1981]) comes closer to it in his incorporation of Karl-Heinz Wortzene's "First Law of Wordstruct": "Language is the spatiodynamic activity of letters to reproduce— an activity which defines functionally the creation of language." Truhlar, in paraphrasing Wortzene's Second Law, states "'mirror' type letters have the power of perpetual motion thru time & space creating language," but fails to take this literally. This failure leads him to question "whether a permanent accomplishment in language is desirable." We have already seen in PS 34 the movement of large airborne letters over North America pointing to the possibility of an alphabetically richer past of which our written language is but a shadow. It is this historical reality which I wish to address in this paper, but I have sketched some points of agreement & disagreement with the Onto-Geneticists because of the relevance of their researches to my own. I will not be distracted by their time-travel theorizing (see my own PS 10 in *Zygal*) or the fate of Henri La Pursse (an alternate explanation exists which I will mention at the end of this paper). Instead I will focus on those facts I have been able to uncover re: both the nature of the alphabet & the alphabet cult, & the real meaning of "a permanent accomplishment in language."

II

The first thing that strikes one in studying a map of Manitoba, & something that appears insignificant if not completely whimsical, is the existence of a kind of *anglais patois*, a strange pidgin English, visible as whole sentences as one begins to read the adjacent towns in the various sequences the connecting ley lines suggest. Some of the sentences I have been unable, at this writing, to fully decipher. Many, in fact. For example:

> Assessippi shellmouth dropmore tummel.
> Deepdale makaroff san clara boggy creek.

A tentative translation of the first sentence would suggest that it refers to some shell-mouthed creature that created tumult in the writer/speaker's world thru the destruction of something (?). Sorting thru the word drift, visible thru dropped letters, sonic changes in configuration & the running together of words & phrases, we see, in the first word/phrase, the suggestion of a call to assess the slippage or damage, perhaps thru the application of a formula involving *pi*. Here, too, the *pi* shell (circle) coupled with mouth points to a possible letter O, or some similar, but forgotten, glyph. The second sentence seems nonsensical but it is possible that I have not yet found its proper order.

But these are just two of the sentences[4] this landuage[5] generates. Nonetheless they are representative of the dream-like quality that permeates the naming. One moves from town to town reading strange fragmentary texts that ripple as if viewed beneath the lost waters of Lake Agassiz. But I wish to focus in this particular essay, which is, after all, only an approach to this whole question, on three particular groupings, two from an area some 200 miles west of Winnipeg, & the third 100 or so south-west.

1) "Minnedosa clanwilliam."
This first sentence, even its possible variants, seems to have one fairly clear meaning:

```
Many⁶ (of those?) (claim) (we'll)  i am.
      (dozen?)    (clan)  (will)
```

The message is interpretable in two ways: 1) "A large number of things &/or objects will 'i am' (i.e. create [themselves? something else?])"; or 2) "A large number of things &/or objects are in the process of creating (themselves or something else)." Here, written in the landscape of Manitoba, is the proof of Wortzene's "First Law of Wordstruct" *recorded at a time that predates Wortzene's formulation*! But I anticipate myself slightly, for tho one could say that the things &/or objects referred to are letters, what proof do we have? Let us continue to the second sentence, a more problematic, & in some ways more interesting, text.

2) "Erickson rackham onanole wasagaming."

```
(airy kiss)  (on) (rock)(he'm)        (O'll)(was)  (a gaming)
(Erick's)    (&)  (rack)(hum)   on an (O L) (w as) (a came in)
(air sticks)      (Ra come)           (old)
```

My preferred reading of these possible variants is "Airy kiss & Ra come on an old W as A came in." This hymn-like, or possibly narrative religious, text points to sky phenomena: the movement of large letters over Manitoba, letters which the gods rode. And even the other variant readings hint at fabulous possibilities. "Erick's on a rock, he'm on an O L W as [or O'll was] a gaming." Or: "Air sticks on a rock [or 'rack'], hum on an old W [or, again, 'O L W'] as A came in [or, indeed, 'a gaming']." In the first variant Erick (possibly related to Viking travels in some way) sits on a rock, & this could be viewed in the tradition of the stone/cloud water/sky landscape rimes, since the next statement, "he'm on an O L W" (or even "O'll"), points to the rock as being in reality a letter form, or forms, & therefore related to

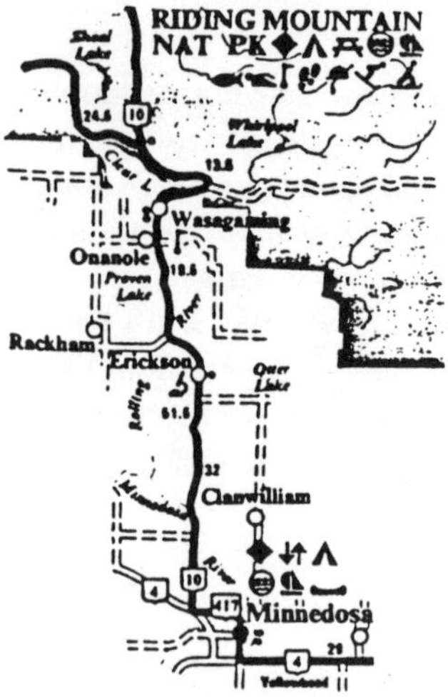

the above discussed airborne letters. Intriguing is the additional notion that this forms part of a game strategy ("as a gaming" or "was a gaming") or that an additional letter, an A, "came in" to sight at that time (also relating to the possible game strategy). As in the previous sentence, the notion that someone (god or human) can control concrete manifestations is put forward &, in the case at hand, is specifically attached to alphabetic forms. The control device may in fact be the "airy kiss" which invokes Ra, invokes the airborne letters, & a ritual, not delineated, which is played out even as a game is played out. In the second variant, "air sticks" on a rock or rack. The invisible & ineffable sticks to, finds form in, the rock/cloud, the cloud as rack on which meaning's hung. This translation of the ineffable into the solid, the invisible into active participant in the visible, takes the form of a song or hum. As we will see, the next grouping picks up on this theme.

3) "Windygates morden winkler altona."

```
                       (wins clear)       (tune(s))
Windy gates more than  (wrinkles)    all  (tone(s))
                                         (A  tones (?))
```

The "gates" referred to are conceptually equivalent to the sky. The sky is the gate, is a number of gates, thru which the wind blows & thru which the letters enter the earth, & are invoked (as in the previous sequence) into presence in this world. They are the windy gates, the divine breath, the "airy kiss" which brings the alphabet, & hence language, into being. The middle of the sequence is problematical since the meanings that are generated are antithetical. "The sky more than wins clear" or "more than wrinkles." Are the alphabet cultists warning us that in every transmission a garbling, or wrinkling, takes place? Or are they celebrating the clarity with which the gods speak, the sky as godpage on which the letters of the godtext form? The concluding part of the phrase, in all its meanings, points to a possible sonic element or, at least, the transmission of texts to be sung.

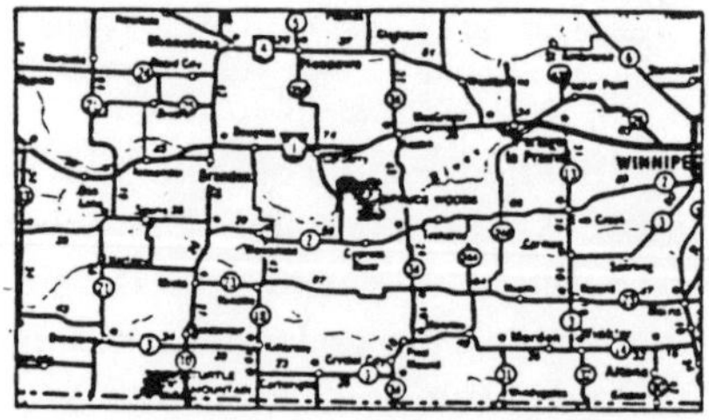

This connects with the Hopi myth of Palongawhoya, the sky writing his text or, as in the opening invocation of John— "In the beginning was the Word: the Word was with God and the Word was God"— in which no distinction is made between print & sound, making it difficult to determine whether the "Word" manifested itself visually or sonically.

Certainly in all three of the texts I have developed here the "wrinkling" referred to in the last one takes place. J.R. Pierce (in his *Symbols, Signals and Noise* [New York: Harper & Row, 1961]), while discussing the general problem of noise in any medium, or channel, of communication, says: "When the recipient receives a message over a noisy channel, he knows what message he has received, but he cannot ordinarily be sure what message was transmitted. Thus, his uncertainty as to what message the sender chose is not completely resolved even on the receipt of a message."[7] Thus a question here would be whether the encoding of the message includes a doubling of messages, a deliberate wrinkling in order to multiply the possibility of at least one message getting thru. Pierce comments on this:

> In order to encode messages for error-free transmission over noisy channels, long sequences of symbols must be lumped together and encoded as one supersymbol.

This block encoding adds redundancies to nonredundant messages to ensure as accurate a transmission as possible over a noisy channel. There is no noisier channel than time. The years wear away at the transmitted bits & wrinkle any message. Thus, to transmit thru history to an unknown receiver/reader in the future, how do you ensure the message getting thru? I believe one method to have been a doubling up of content so that even when the wrinkling took place, as it clearly did in the texts we examined, much if not all of the word sequence is received. But a second problem confronted the alphabet cultists. How do you transmit thru history a language which may be unfamiliar to your receiver, in characters which may be equally unfamiliar? Pierce addresses this problem from a slightly different angle in his chapter on "Information Theory and Art":

> To be appreciated by an audience, art must be intelligible to the audience...to be appreciated art must be in a language familiar to the audience. Some artists adopt a language taught to their audience by earlier masters... Other artists teach something of a new language to their audience, as the impressionists did. Certainly, the language of art changes with time, and we should be grateful to the artists who teach us new words.

It was the latter strategy which the alphabet cultists adopted. The scale of the project is astounding: transmitting letters thru the centuries till the

Phoenicians finally took them up. Then the subsequent chance operations till English, as a language, emerged. Only then could there be a hope that the messages they had coded in the landscape would be readable. Thus it is not chance, or mere whimsy, that produced these town names, but a system of prodded & forced responses undoubtedly much like the systems magicians use to force us to pick the book they want us to pick.

But what other clues do we have, what other signs that point us towards this prescient alphabet cult in Manitoba?[8] Let us move on to a second set of clues the map of Manitoba reveals.

III

We have already seen how in the wrinkling of the messages the alphabet cult[9] encoded a degree of obfuscation took place that has made it difficult for contemporary readers to recognize the Manitoba texts for what they are. The effects of this wrinkling are present on another level of the code, a level of disappearance that in itself defines some of the activities of the cult. In northern Manitoba on the Saskatchewan border two other key messages appear: Flin Flon & The Pas. What immediately strikes one in reading these is, in both cases, the elided letters. Obviously The Pas should more properly be The Past & Flin Flon— Fling Flong. But what happened to the Pas'*t*? And what happened to the Flin & Flon *g*s? These, as the title of this essay suggests, were the questions I actually began with. But the texts we have already dealt with, texts which I "read" only after addressing myself to digging up a solution to the mystery of the missing Pas *t*, are vital to an understanding of the probable solution I came to.

I believe these two place-names to be the supersymbols the cultists encoded, the rosetta stone they established for an unknown reader/receiver in the millennia ahead. Once understood as such the message is astoundingly simple & clear. The choice of basic yet key words on which a deliberate elision was practised was a stroke of genius. The *g* of Flin*g* is flung away. The *t* of Pas*t* is left behind. Hence Flin & hence The Pas. The message refers directly to the wrinkling effect of the transmission. Flin*g* was flung, was shot out thru time, The Pas*t* (which was the present) hurled towards the present (which was then future). And a simple formula is derivable from the word structures. Flong is an obvious redundancy added to a nonredundant message. As long as one of them survived the message would get thru. It is probable there was once an additional redundancy in Fling Flong & that The Past was once part of a similar block encoding (possibly Pas Tim Bac or some equivalent super-symbol).[10] In any case only the Pas of Past survives. And in both The Pas & the nonredundant & redundant portions of Flin Flon, the original code word presents only a fraction (3/4 & 4/5) of the whole word. I would like to reiterate here that when I said, only a moment ago, "only the Pas of Past survives," that that is the message I was pushed to take out of it— forced, as it were, by the original encoders who deliberately elided the final *t*. Reading in the found sequence of the place-names, & in the order English as a language takes, the simple formula derivable from this construction could be written as follows:

$$R = M - \left(\frac{W_1 - B}{W_1} + \frac{W_2 - B}{W_2} \cdots\cdots \frac{W_n - B}{W_n} \right)$$

where R equals the received message, W the transmitted element, and 1, 2, etc. the individual variation in a transmitted sequence thru to the nth & final element in the sequence, & B the smallest unit in each transmitted element, with M as the original message sent. Thus any reading of a three-element message must assume a minimum one element loss. Conversely, any transmission of a four element message must assume only three elements would be received. And this formula represents minimal loss figures only! Hence the wrinkling effect observed in the texts discussed in part II. I would take this a step further, however, & declare that the cultists have deliberately wrinkled *all* their messages in order to increase the amount of content in each one, much as James Joyce did in *Finnegans Wake*. Thus we would have to assume there were many more redundancies in the original transmissions than currently exist since the only way to convey such complex information thru the noisy channel of history is to slow the transmission down thru repetition. Interestingly enough, this probably means that the original texts read like a cross between James Joyce & Gertrude Stein, the great streams of modernist prose— texts which combined Stein's insistence with Joyce's multiple layerings. This realization coupled with the cracking of The Pas/Flin Flon code was what allowed me to translate the texts in part II. The location of these key words in the upper left corner of the page-shaped map of Manitoba[11] supports my thesis that they are the entry point to the encoded text that exists there. The main work, the complete translation of Manitoba in order to understand the full content of what the alphabet cult was transmitting, lies ahead of me. But some clues exist even at this stage, & it is these few clues that bring me back to the questions this essay set out to answer— the nature of the alphabet, of the alphabet cult, & the real meaning of "a permanent accomplishment in language."

IV

We have already seen certain things about the alphabet & the alphabet cult. It appears (as already demonstrated in PS 34) that in the distant past whole alphabets were visible in the sky. We would assume them to be either actual floating letters or perhaps cloud shapes, tho it is certainly possible they took the form of meteorite showers (& here the reference to "rock" in the second sentence/text dealt with becomes intriguing), or even the slow shift of the pole star over millennia & the change it brought about in constellations. What is definite is that it was a sky phenomenon & it was visible. Further, it seems there were rituals & games associated with the invoking of these letter forms & even a hint that the gods rode them. It also seems they were willed into being by the tribes or, at least, that their appearance coincided with certain powerful tribal rituals. It is possible too that some kind of creature(s) preyed on these letter forms causing their virtual extinction (only H's & L's visible today). This much we know from the texts I have deciphered. It tells us that the alphabet had a visible existence in the world; that the few proofs we see in the present (alphabet-shaped rocks & plants,[12] letter movements over North America, etc.) reference a richer, visible past; that its survival as a print code is due largely to the existence of an alphabet cult, the concerted effort of an unknown number of beings. About the alphabet cult we know far less. What we do know we must deduce from their activities. Certainly the sheer immensity of their task suggests the value which they placed on their as yet undeciphered content, a content so important they were willing to wait the thousands of years it would take to will a group of reader/receivers into existence.[13] "Many dozen clan will 'i am.'" But clans of what? Who were the alphabet cult? Not human surely? For if human what need of a human audience in some far future? No, they were something else, some other life form intermediary between gods & men— analogous, perhaps, to the position saints came to occupy. We know the gods were more present to them & we know they went to great lengths to encode some message into Manitoba. There is reason to believe that some of their race, at least one, lived into the 1930s.[14] Beyond that nothing has been known.

But why Manitoba? Why such an incredible encoding in such an unlikely spot? There are three more clues present in the map of Manitoba & these will take us as far as we can go in this particular quest at this particular point in time. These clues are the place-names Hnausa, Hecla & Gimli.

In Ms. Charity Lewis' & Dr. R.W. Sanderson's translation of "Royal Cylinder 2957.345" (published as *The Institute of Hṃṃrian Studies Occasional*

Papers No. 3 [Institute of Hmmrian Studies, Toronto] : 1978 (?); reissued in *Open Letter* 4th ser. 6/7 [Winter 1980-81]), King Tzln II's address to Xrtznqrh, leader of the priests at Ntzxrtzh, Tzln says "As naked children, O Xrtznqrh, my people fled the Three Cities of Hnsdnnr in the ancient time, when the Time of Great Cold descended upon us." In Sanderson's earlier translation of the "Cylinder of Histories" from the Humber River Site of the Snnrian empire, Sanderson tentatively identified "the Lands of Cold" as the Wisconsin Glacier. But this is, I think, vastly mistaken. We are talking of a period circa 9,300 B.C. Is it not more logical to look for the Three Cities of Hnsdnnr in a more northerly clime even than Wisconsin?

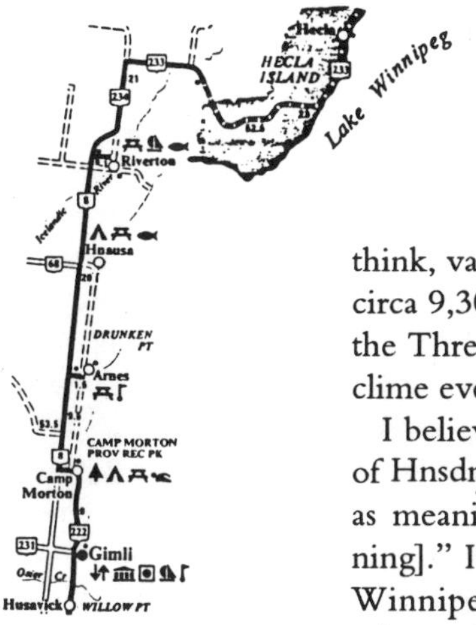

I believe Hnausa to be one of the Three Cities of Hnsdnnr. I would tentatively translate its name as meaning: "Hn[sdnnr] was A [i.e. the beginning]." Its location, on the western edge of Lake Winnipeg midway between Gimli & Hecla, whose significance I will explain momentarily, only serves to strengthen my claim.

To understand my second point/clue we only need to look briefly at the history of Manitoba. In 1875-76, 1500 Icelanders emigrated to Manitoba after a volcanic eruption in Iceland destroyed their farms. Many of them settled at Gimli, Hnausa & Hecla Island. In the language of Iceland, Gimli means "home of the gods." This was actually the first of these three clues that I discovered, but takes on its true significance once we realize Hnausa for what it is. Gimli is the second of the Three Cities of Hnsdnnr. I believe the Icelandic settlers were aware of traditions & realities we have not been aware of.

For the third clue let us again examine R. W. Sanderson's Hmmrian researches. In his *Great Hmmr: The Story of the World's Oldest Civilization* (London: Penguin, 1977— as quoted in *Canadian "Pataphysics*), Sanderson states that present day Pelee Island is the holy isle of Hmmr where Xrtzh & his nine companions, the Ptntr, arrived long after the Lords of Cold destroyed the City of Gods. But why Pelee? Why this point of land & this particular island? In a tourist description of Hecla Island included in *Canadian Book of the Road* (Montreal: *Reader's Digest*, 1979) the following sentence appears:

At the southern end of Hecla, marshes support Canada, blue and snow geese, whistling swans, bald eagles, and some 15 species of ducks.

I believe this marsh & the extensive wild fowl that inhabited it found its rime for the descendants of the inhabitants of Hecla & Hecla Island, the third of the Three Cities of Hnsdnnr, in Point Pelee's marsh & the hundreds of species that inhabit it. For the distant ancestors of Xrtzh & the Ptntr were sent forth "with the command that they must return and rebuild the City in all its glory." And it is my belief that Xrtzh chose a site, an island on a large inland lake near extensive marshes, that matched the garbled descriptions in the fragmentary texts of his own history. Xrtzh thot he was home in the landscape his ancestors had been forced to abandon. Thus was Hmmrian civilization & the Snnrian empire founded a thousand miles or more to the south-east of the original godhome.

My point here is not to argue Sanderson's locating of Hnsdnnr in Wisconsin (I believe I have demonstrated three substantial reasons for placing it on the western edge of Lake Winnipeg with Gimli, Hnausa & Hecla, on Hecla Island, as the Three Cities). My purpose in making these identifications has been to establish the identity of the alphabet cult's first recruits & to date its beginnings to roughly 12,000 B.C., when the advancing ice-age first notified the Manitoba civilization of the necessity of a truly long range plan if their culture & its heritage were to survive. These were the beings that founded the Hmmrian civilization, who began the alphabet cult & who were, themselves, regarded as gods. It is possible, of course, that Gimli, Hnausa & Hecla represent inter-ice-age or late ice-age sites of a constantly retrenching civilization.[15] But this lies outside the scope of this present inquiry & begins to encroach on other areas of research I am not really qualified to comment on. The identification I have made here is not final by any means, but it is, at long last, a starting point. The Hmmrian language[16] is not the language the alphabet cult's originators wrote their original texts in.[17] Rather, they began a 14,000-year project which only now, with my discoveries & those of the Linguistic Onto-Geneticists, is reaching some kind of fruition. The "permanent accomplishment in language" begins to become clear. I suspect, from the reference to the shell-mouthed creature, as well as other vague hints in the place names Souris, Shilo & Bagot, & the encoded sequence "Arden keyes ogilvie gladstone," that the living letter forms became an ecologically endangered species. I believe that the civilization that founded the alphabet cult encoded for the future a history of their civilization & its accomplishments, a history of the living alphabet & of the gods of their civilization, gods who used the skypage & its alphabets to speak to them, the utterers of the urtext. I believe, as I have already outlined & provided some tentative proofs for, that they were willing to take the 14,000 years or more it might take to pass on their heritage &, further, that they knew exactly how long it would take, exactly how far & thru how noisy a channel their message would have to be transmitted. This statement (& Truhlar rightly identifies "statement" as the "permanent accomplishment in language") is there to be decoded by the receivers it was intended for. The phrase "a permanent accomplishment in language," so carefully used by Wortzene, refers not to a desired goal (as Truhlar tends to interpret it) but rather to something pre-existent, a permanent accomplishment nested in the language as something to be decoded. Wortzene too must have discovered the alphabet cult.

V

I have sketched in this paper some of the preliminary findings from my alphabet research in Manitoba. What proofs I have been able to make I have proffered. I know certain areas must still appear weakly supported, but I have clearly labelled the speculative as speculative & have included such things here only to flesh out for you the direction in which my thoughts are moving. Given the time &, hopefully, an adequate source of funds, I hope to find new proofs in the mapped landscape of Manitoba, the many to be, the infinite possibilities & wrinklings of meaning.

NOTES

1. (At right.) Detail from Ra Ma Da cult map used in Probable System 18 (in *Art Facts*).

2. The true connection between Wo & Mo & the reason for the numberless tels associated with the latter & the almost total lack of probable sites associated with the former, is worth exploring further.

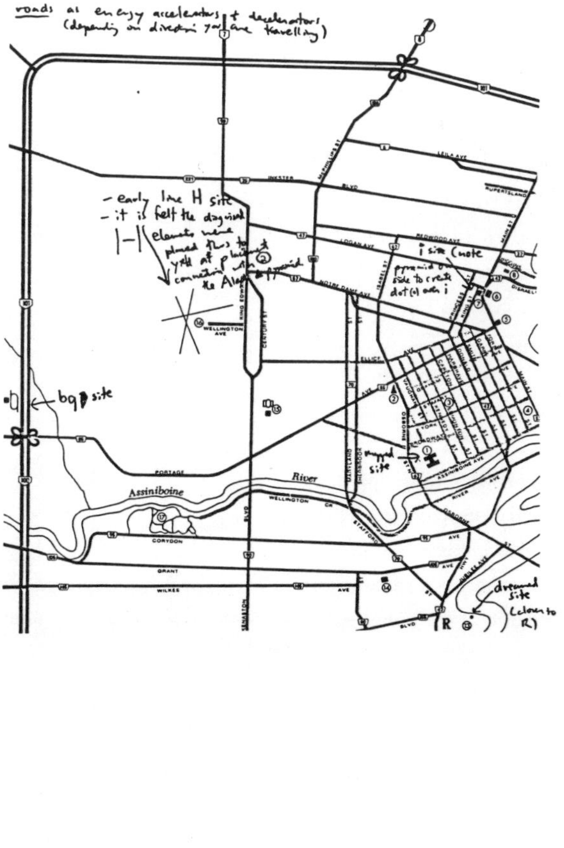

3. (Below.) Detail from the as yet unpublished Probable System 34:

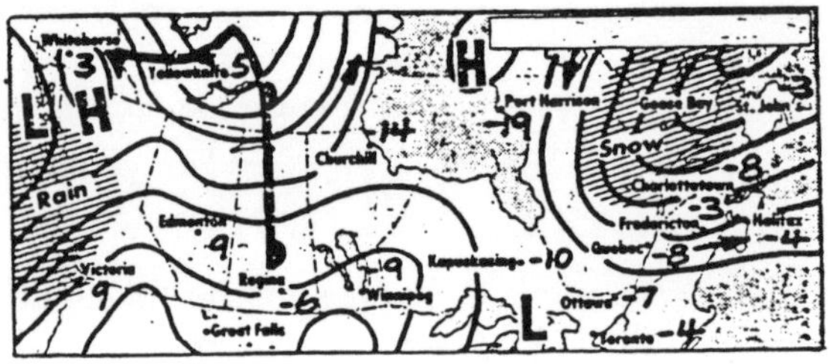

February 20— 4 H's sighted. One south-east of Whitehorse, one over Hudson Bay northwest of Port Harrison, two south of the Canadian border.

4. En says?, i.e., the says of "En." In a future Probable System I will study the preponderance of two letter godnames as in Da, Wo, Mo, Ma, Ra & En.

5. This portmanteau word is used to differentiate from the *air say* the floating letters generate (& hence "heresy" [a topic I shall return to]).

6. It is possible that "Minne" should be read "mini," particularly if "dosa" translates "dozen." But this does not change the essential content of the phrase, merely the size of the event.

7. (At right.) In the autumn of 1980, while running my calculations for determining the square root of logic (PS 9) thru the Coach House press computer (in preparation for its inclusion in *As Elected* [Vancouver: Talonbooks, 1981]), the computer fed me back the following calculations which I have been unable, at this writing, to decipher, but which correctly identify the relationship between "noise" & Heisenberg's "Principle of Uncertainty." It is published here as an alternative version of PS 9.

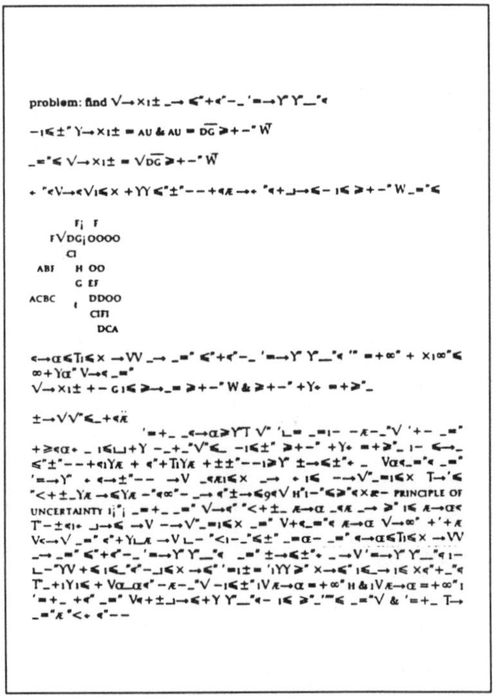

8. "Manitoba" I have tentatively translated as "Many to be," i.e. to become, to go forth and multiply.

9. Thruout this essay I am using "alphabet cult" to denote both the originators of the Manitoba texts & the "people" they entrusted with the maintenance of the project. There is little doubt in my mind that these were two completely different groups. From a recent (Friday, 13 November, 1981) conversation with Prof. M. Dean, I gather that D. Penhale has made discoveries re: La Pursse that may bear out the contention I make a little later in this essay.

10. Pas Tim Bac would have been Past Time Back. As an instance of this supersymbol's existence, Timmins, Ontario, presents a possible proof. It relates, too, to Hmmrian Studies, an area we will be touching on in the fourth part of this essay.

11. The shape of Manitoba is, I believe, another example of the alphabet cult's ability to "force" a response— behavioural engineering on a colossal scale. Language (because I believe what I am saying applies to more than English) is the largest visible monument of a forgotten civilization.

12. See my own *As Elected* for Kim Ondaatje's excellent photo of an H-shaped tree in the Nass Valley of Northern British Columbia. Also relevant to this particular point is Adrian Fortesque's "Ambulatory Signification: A Letter" (in *Canadian "Pataphysics*) particularly in light of the unintentional pun in the title, which I believe reveals the deeper truth behind the granitification Fortesque so observantly noted.

13. This very point deserves expansion. Manitoba (as I stated in note 11 by implication) is not the only site, nor is English the only language the alphabet cult worked in. But what can one researcher do? I am already straining my resources in an attempt to deal with this one site. Fortunately documentation exists on another key site, Bracebridge (& here the obvious message, the "Braced Bridge" [& its relationship to Dean's discovery of the bridge over the Amstel River] should be obvious), Ontario, in the form of two articles: Kurt Wurstwagen's "Piccu Carlu: The Muskoka-Maya Connexion" & R. Truhlar's "Report From Piccu Carlu" (in *Canadian "Pataphysics*). Tho both misinterpret the facts as set before them, imagining a taboo against writing in the Muskokan site, Wurstwagen frames the correct question when he asks "Could not a writing have existed in a form other than that of an incisive act?" His discovery of Bracebridge Site 37D, major in itself, is typically misinterpreted as a ground writing when of course it is a sky tracing. Had he rethought Schrödinger's translation of the stone Book of Mool, which he quotes, the clues were all there: "whose page is no page whose words are no words, whose tongue is not tongue but the tongue of stone through which speech dies and becomes eternity..." Stone is also "s tone," the "airy kiss," & "speech dies" the "speeched eyes" thru which eternity, & the gods, are glimpsed. Every stone rimes the sky in some way. To be fair, neither Schrödinger nor Wurstwagen had access to the principles of layering & redundancy that the Manitoba texts revealed to us. I also agree with Wurstwagen's more significant discovery, the Proto-Mayan glyphs, tho they strike me more as steps along the road to the Phoeni-

cian alphabet, a record of one of the intermediary steps in the "forcing" technique of the alphabet cultists (indeed I think many "untranslatable" languages are simply this, a discarded dead-end on the road to the present). And it is obvious Wurstwagen has made the basic connection when he states: "Here the Muskokan mind learned how reading must always precede a writing, how the human telos is an ur-literacy, how man is destined to read and nature's 'function' to have already written." Truhlar's companion paper contains a fascinating proof of my thesis on the meaning of the proto-Mayan glyphs when he points to "an unconscious cultural structuration of a nonreferential macro- and micro-syntax involving both sub-linguistic glyph and topographic cypher," earmarks of a culture "forced" by the alphabet cult along a certain route. Both papers are brilliant & should be read in the light of the Manitoba texts.

14. See D. Penhale's "From Linguistic Onto-Genetics to Euclidean Projectivist Linguistics," R. Truhlar's "The Crisis of the Cultural Masterwork in Linguistic Onto-Genetics," & Steven Smith's "Letter to L'Institut Onto-Génetique" (all in *Canadian "Pataphysics*). All three opt for an improbable time-travel solution when what is happening, of course, is the expression of a group will of incredible strength over uncounted millennia. It needs no time-travel fabrication when there is a system of belief & fanatic followers of that system. Far more interesting is the question of human disguise. But that leads us down too many paths extraneous to the central argument of this brief essay.

15. Particularly since, as presently located, they would have been roughly in the middle of Lake Agassiz. But alternate explanations of this phenomenon do exist, the simplest of which is the already discussed revelation that the founders of the alphabet cult were not human.

16. It is interesting to note in the various papers Sanderson allowed to be reprinted in the Winter 1980-81 issue of *Open Letter*, how the Hṃṃrian names are almost entirely constructed of consonants, & to contrast that with R. Truhlar's statement in his essay "Towards A Constructivist Theory of Linguistic Onto-Genetics" that "primitive or tribal societies were based on languages that had a predominance of vowels among words." It is my own belief that this separation was part of the preparation to transmit consonants & vowels separately thru the noisy channel of time—a stereo signal beamed towards its true receiver in the 20th century.

17. They chose to imitate the skytext (see Wurstwagen on Bracebridge 37D). They were the originators of the chronodynamic word & spatiodynamic speech. Indeed this is the point at which Truhlar & I are in complete agreement. Our researches complement & underline each other.

Kite 4

For David McFadden

(November/72)

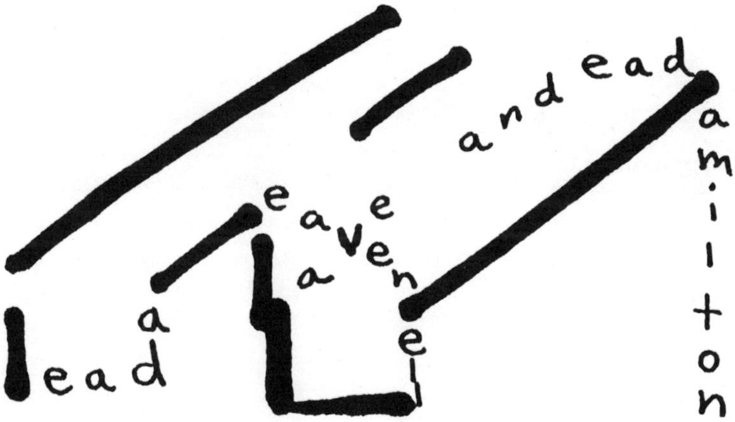

Sketching 4

(Richard Truhlar reading, June 19/81)

1
"a house perhaps"

or how's 'at?

"cringing backwards in a mirror"

pal in dromic
in the gnomic language

engaged

2
"shorter than we remember"

dis appointment or
meeting

                    "one of us is cheating"

i.e. reading

the questions in advance

3
"we believe we are out there"

listening

the mind's wedged
in between the ears
here
        where we hear or
speak

au

au

     thordience

4
"the silence of space surrounding things"

Kite 5

(November/72)

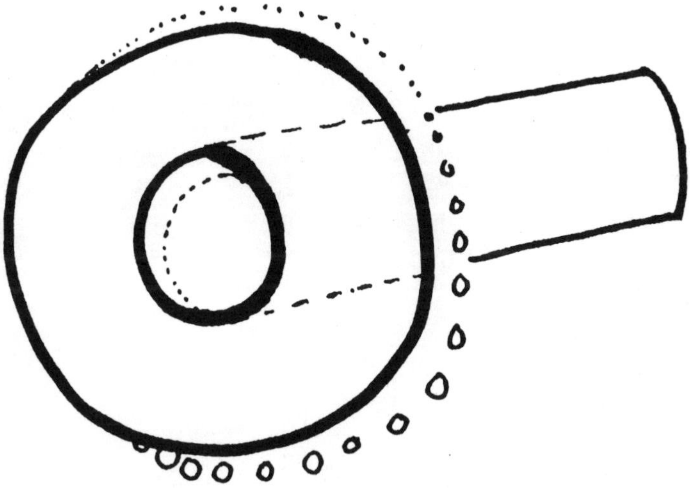

Studies in the Book Machine 6
(July 31/82)

Page 91

(If you rip it out
is it still page 91?)

Studies in the Book Machine 7
(July 31/82)

——————————— Page 92

(If you rip it out does
that make *this* page
page 91 or does it stay
page 93? I.e. it's blank
& not significant in the
sequence. What is
"significance" in a
sequence?)

A Winter's Tale (for Rafael)

After Jiri Valoch

M: snow?
W: no
M: o
W: snow?
M: no
W: o
M: snow?
W: no
M: o
W: snow?
M: no
W: o
M: snow?
W: no
M: o
W: snow?
M: now!
W & M: o

Sine
(Horizon 17)
(1987)

68' 30" Point in *Patria II*
(For Murray Schafer Collaboration)

self' s one
unmoving
faster than the mind

senses lag

self runs ahead
unmoving
outruns pursuit

out of self
the breath the
life of
all things

.

unmoving/moves
far away/near
within/outside
ALL

Love Song 6

For Ellie on her Birthday

(November 19/73, 12:02 a.m.)

all the ways that i had thot of loving
filled as i can be with such conceits
disappear in the face of you
the place you do take in my heart

all the awkwardness that i feel in phrasing
poems that speak of my loving for you
caught as they do catch in a moment's saying
so that i feel embarrassed or arrogant
hesitating where i should be sure
are nothing when i hold you
unable to speak
                    reach over the years of our separate growing
older together
                    measured in time
we note startled
no closer to knowing "what love is"
except that respect
                        that continual wonder
i still dissemble before
more in love with you than ever

Studies in the Book Machine 10

(December 2/82)

DIRECTIONAL
BIAS
2

The World: A History Well Lost

ACT I Scene 1

(The palace of Cleopatra in Alexandria, a Sphinx stage left, votive altar to Isis stage right. Enter Antony 1, walking with a disturb'd motion.)

ANTONY 1:

They tell me 'tis my birthday, and I'll keep it
With double pomp of sadness.
'Tis what the day deserves which gave me breath.

(The light still clears, and a mass of colour between the Sphinx's great paws defines itself as a girl lying motionless. A man comes from the south with stealing steps, and halts, lost in contemplation, opposite the left flank of the Sphinx. The girl is hidden from him by its massive shoulder. Antony 1 is unaware of either of them.)

CAESAR 1:

Hail, Sphinx: salutation from Julius Caesar! In the little world
yonder, Sphinx, my place is as high as yours in this great desert;
only I wander, and you sit still; I conquer, and you endure;
I work and wonder, you watch and wait; I look up and am dazzled,
look down and am darkened, look round and am puzzled, whilst your
eyes never turn from looking out— out of the world— to the
lost region— the home from which we have strayed.

ANTONY 1:

(Still unaware of the others.)

Why was I rais'd the meteor of the world,
Hung in the skies, and blazing as I travel'd
Till all my fires were spent, and then cast downward
To be trod out by Caesar?

(Throws himself down.)

Lie there, thou shadow of an emperor;
The place thou pressest on thy mother earth
Is all thy empire now; now it contains thee;
Some few days hence and then 'twill be too large,
When thou'rt contracted in thy narrow urn,
Shrunk to a few old ashes.

CLEOPATRA 2:

(Who has wakened, and peeped cautiously from her nest to see who is speaking.)

Old gentleman.

(Both Caesar & Antony 1 start violently. Caesar clutches his sword. Antony remains lying face down.)

CAESAR 1:

Immortal gods!

ANTONY 1:

I'm angry.

CLEOPATRA 2:

Old gentleman: don't run away.

CAESAR 1:

(Stupefied.)

"Old gentleman: don't run away"!!! This! to Julius Caesar!

ANTONY 1:

I would be private; leave me.

CLEOPATRA 2:

Old gentleman.

ANTONY 1:

Where have you learnt that answer? Who am I?

CAESAR 1:

Sphinx, you presume on your centuries. I am younger than you, though your voice is but a girl's voice as yet.

(Flourish. Enter Antony 2, Cleopatra 3.)

CLEOPATRA 3:

If it be love indeed, tell me how much.

ANTONY 2:

There's beggary in the love that can be reckoned.

CLEOPATRA 3:

I'll set a bourn how far to be beloved.

CLEOPATRA 2:

(Glancing towards the back of the stage where Antony 2 & Cleopatra 3 stand.)

Climb up here, quickly; or the others will come and eat you.

CAESAR 1:

(Running forward past the Sphinx's shoulder, and seeing her.)

A child at its breast! A divine child!

ANTONY 1:

(Standing with head bowed— he does not see Cleopatra 2 or Caesar but talks to them.)

Now thou hast seen me, art thou satisfy'd?
For, if a friend, thou hast beheld enough,
And, if a foe, too much.

CAESAR 1:

(Totally unaware of Antony I as is Cleopatra 2.)

Who are you?

CLEOPATRA 2:

Cleopatra, Queen of Egypt.

ANTONY 1:

(Thinking the question addressed to him answers simultaneously.)

Antony,
Well, thou wilt have it, like a coward, fled,
Fled while his soldiers fought, fled first,
Thou long'st to curse me, and I give thee leave.
I know thou cam'st prepar'd to rail.

ANTONY 2:

(Who has become aware of the conversation at the front of the stage & gestures angrily.)

Grates me! The sum.

CLEOPATRA 3:

Nay, hear them, Antony. Who knows
If the scarce-bearded Caesar have not sent
His pow'rful mandate to you, "Do this, or this;
Take in that kingdom, and enfranchise that.
Perform't, or else we damn thee."

ANTONY 2:

How, my love?

CLEOPATRA 3:

Hear it, Antony.

CAESAR 1:

(To himself.)

What a dream! What a magnificent dream!

(He climbs up on the Sphinx with her.)

ANTONY 1:

(Looking up & not seeing anybody.)

Ha, ha, ha, ha!

(Throws himself down on the ground again.)

ANTONY 2:

Let Rome in Tiber melt and the wide arch
Of the ranged empire fall! Here is my space,
Kingdoms are clay: our dungy earth alike
Feeds beast as man.

CLEOPATRA 3:

(Aside to audience.)

I'll seem the fool I am not. Antony
will be himself.

ANTONY 2:

Let's not confound the time with conference harsh.
There's not a minute of our lives should stretch
Without some pleasure now. What sport to-night?

CLEOPATRA 3:

Hear them.

ANTONY 2:

Fie, wrangling queen!
No messages but thine, and all alone
To-night we'll wander through the streets and note
The qualities of people. Come, my queen;
Last night you did desire it.— Speak not to us.

(Exeunt Antony 2 & Cleopatra 3.)

CLEOPATRA 2:

I'm glad you have come: I was very lonely.

CAESAR 1:

What are you doing here at this time of night? Do you live here?

Twelve Days in the Gobi: A Real-Time Narrative

DAY 1:	startend
DAY 2:	startddend
DAY 3:	startiddlend
DAY 4:	startmiddleend
DAY 5:	startemiddlecend
DAY 6:	startuemiddlecoend
DAY 7:	startnuemiddleconend
DAY 8:	startinuemiddlecontend
DAY 9:	starttinuemiddlecontiend
DAY 10:	startntinuemiddlecontinend
DAY 11:	startontinuemiddlecontinuend
DAY 12:	startcontinuemiddlecontinueend

Studies in the Book Machine 12
(January 18/83)

Other than these words the information on this page is show thru.

States of Translation

(Found on a blackboard, Medical Science Building,
U of T, October 24/78)

ACUTE

SUB-CLINICAL

LATENT

CHRONIC

SLOW

TRANSFORMED

73' 31" Point in *Patria II*
(For Murray Schafer Collaboration)

TADA SE
SVE ODIGRALA
JEDNO ZADRUGIM!

OD JEDNOM
NAŠO JOJ
SE REVOLVER
U RUCI
I OTVORI
VATRU.

METAK SE
ULOŽIO U
DESNU SLEPOOČICU.

Ta ta to
sweet originality
do y'know they drugged 'im!

Odd do y'know
nasty joy
's a revolver
you reach for it
I'm hot for it
very true.

Me i talk to
you lazy o you'
d as soon let sleeping dogs lie.

TATA TE
SVEET ORIDGNLTY
DYNO THÉDRGDIM!

OD DYNO
NZTE DJOI
SA REVOLVER
U RICFRT
I MOTFRT
VARTRU.

ME TAKTA
U LZEOU
DAZOON LTSLPNGDGSLY.

I.T.A.N.U.T.S. 4
(December/72)

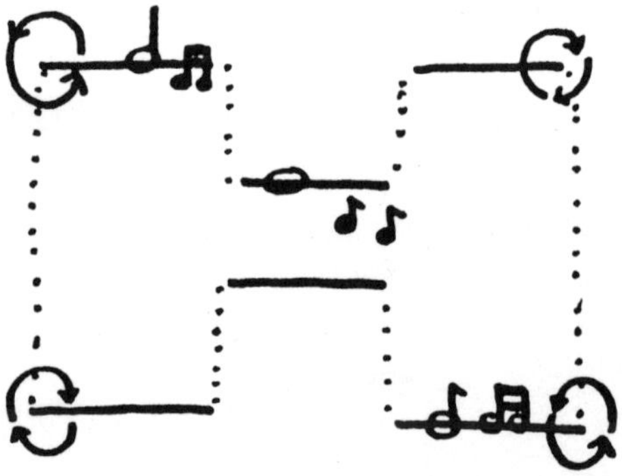

The Many Moods of Dom Sylvester Houedard

Dom Casual ABCDEFGHIJ

Dom Casual: 18 24 30 36 48 60 72

Dom Diag ABCDEFGHIJ

Dom Diagonal: 18 24 30 36 48 60 72

Dom Bld ABCDEFGHIJ

Dom Bold: 18 24 30 36 48 60 72

For Hermann Hesse

HESS

Hess Neobold: 36

This is the Sentence the Wind Blew Here
(Late Fall/73)

```
t       t      t     t
 h       h            h            h
  i  i                    i
   s  s     s
          e  e  e  e   e        e   e e
              n  n         n
                  c
                         w     w
                            d
                              b
                               l
                                     r
```

Tranquill'eau

mer mer mer moi mer mer mer tu mer mer mer

les yeux des poissons

feuille

feuillet

feuilleter

nuage

bloc
ploc

Lines on the Lake

For Wayne Pritchett

(March 18/77)

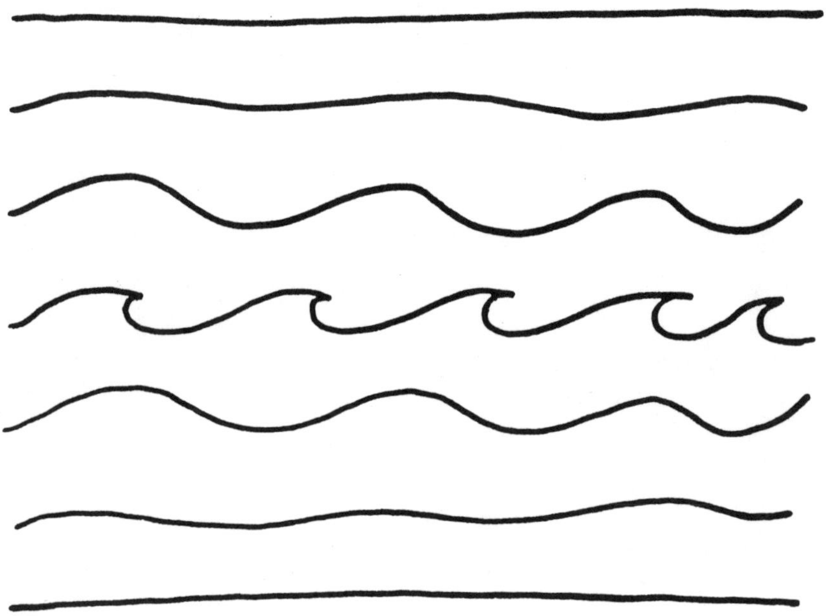

Catalogue of the ”PATAPHYSICAL HARDWARE COMPANY

Founded 1944

bpNichol Prop.

Illustrated

Everything for your imaginary needs.

In response to an overwhelming public demand the "PATAPHYSICAL HARDWARE COMPANY is now offering its services to the general public. For years only the most discriminating 'Pata- & "Pataphysicians were able to obtain goods from our company. But now anyone can enjoy the same imaginative service that's been thrilling those select few all these years. It's easy. Just browse thru our catalogue and select the "Pataphysical item(s) you'd like our skilled clerk(s) to demonstrate. They'll be more than happy to do so.

As a quick glance through the catalogue will show you, items are grouped in logical series for your convenience. Most items are manufactured on our own premises to our justifiably famous exacting standards. In a few cases (clearly labelled in the catalogue) we've stocked "Pataphysical items from other manufacturers that meet our high standards. Naturally we've left gaps in the catalogue for your future needs. Any and all suggestions are welcome.

Imaginatively yours

Proprietor
"PATAPHYSICAL HARDWARE COMPANY

SPEECH & THOT SERIES

1. Speech balloons (O.O.S.) (PS 39)
2. Tho(ugh)t balloons (PS 46)
3. Tho(ugh)t holder (PS 47)
4. Tho(ugh)t suppressants (PS 48)
5.
6.
7.
8.
9.

HARDWARE SERIES

10. Double-ended pencils (O.O.S.) (PS 43)
11. Double-leaded pencils (O.O.S.) (PS 42)
12.
13.
14.
15.
16.
17.
18.
19.

CONCEPTS SERIES

20. Device for generating a poem (O.O.S.)
21. Device for generating a contemporary essay title*
22. Critical Frame of Reference (PS 37)
23.
24.
25. Blank Verse (PS 45)
26. Free Verse (PS 50)
27.
28.
29.

Code: O.O.S. – Out of Stock
N.A. – Not Available
PS – Probable System
*Manufactured by grOnk Press.

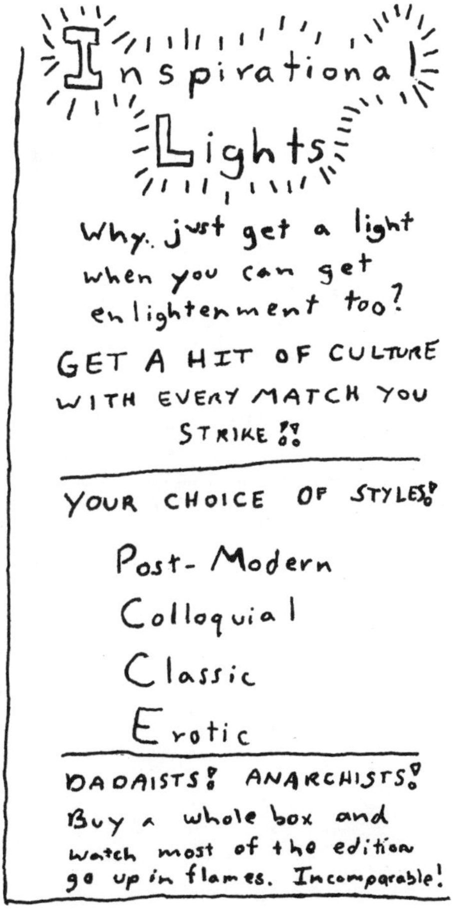

CONSTANTLY ACCUSED OF BEING THOUGHTLESS!

TRY OUR

NEW

Tho(ugh)t Balloons TM

YOU'LL BE HAILED AS THOUGHTFUL FROM NOW ON.

HEY! SERIOUS THINKER!

Having One Of Those Days
Your Thoughts Just Seem To Slip
AWAY?

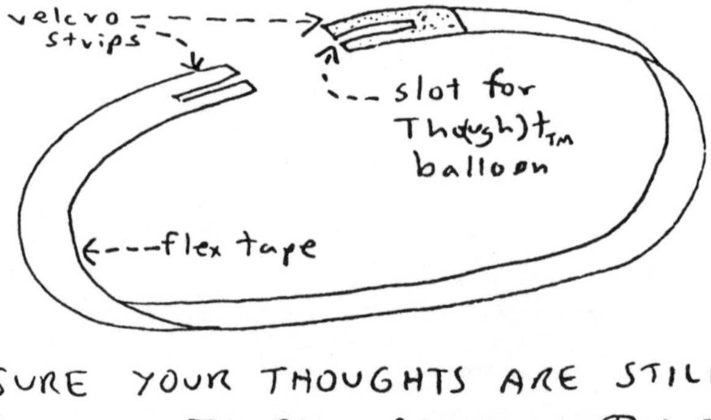

BE SURE YOUR THOUGHTS ARE STILL YOUR OWN WITH OUR PATENTED THOUGHT HOLDERS! THEY'RE FLEXIBLE!!
YOU CAN CHANGE YOUR THOUGHTS IN A MOMENT TOO.

serViCes

30. Open Verse (PS 49)
31. Closed Verse
32.
33.
34.
35.
36.
37.
38.
39.

REFERENCE SERIES*

40. William Carlos Williams (N.A.)
41. Gertrude Stein (N.A.)
42. Francis Ponge (N.A.)
43. Joyce Kilmer (N.A.)
44. William Wordsworth (N.A.)
45. Charles Olson (N.A.)
46.
47.
48.
49.

*Grow-Your-Own-Reference Series is PS 44;
Living-Reference Series is PS 51

PLANNED
for 1987

The "LIVING-REFERENCES-
BRING-EM-BACK-ALIVE"
Series

subject to local laws

COMING
for Spring 1986

The GROW-YOUR-OWN-REFERENCES Series

Wordsworth's Daffodils
Stein's Roses
Olson's Tansy
Ponge's Meadow Grass
Kilmer's Trees

EXPERIENCE THE GREAT REFERENCE'S OF
LITERATURE IN YOUR OWN BACKYARD!!

OWN YOUR VERY OWN
SPEECH BALLOONS

made from
☆ washable ☆
high impact
plastic

2-Sided

so you can talk out of both sides of
your mouth*

ASK ABOUT OUR VERY REASONABLE SPEECH WRITING SERVICES (you provide the pen tho)

* you'll have to purchase two if you want to talk out of both sides at once.

Poetry
L♡vers

get your
GENUINE BRAND
BLANK
VERSE

"Non blanker or your money back"

NOW !!

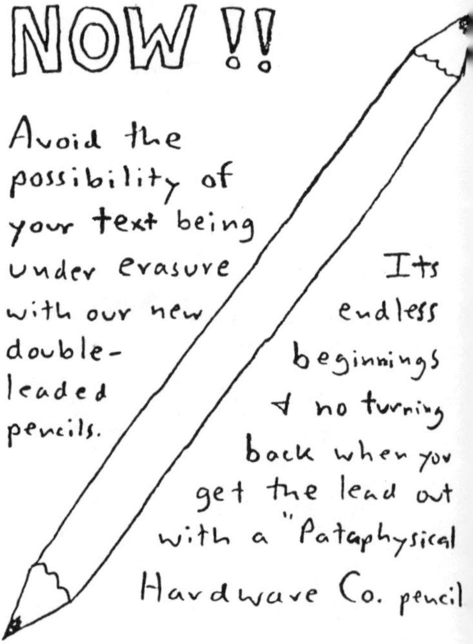

Avoid the possibility of your text being under erasure with our new double-leaded pencils.

Its endless beginnings & no turning back when you get the lead out with a "Pataphysical Hardware Co. pencil

REGULAR USERS OF THIS CATALOGUE ARE USED TO OUR JOKE-OF-THE-ISSUE FEATURE. WE OFFER FREE MERCHANDISE IN EXCHANGE FOR ANY JOKE USED. THIS JOKE IS FROM Triste Zava, Age 12:

THANKS Triste!

NON SERIES

50.
51.
52.
53.
54.
55.
56.
57.
58.
59.

LEISURE LIVING SERIES

60.
61. Plaster de Paris (PS 40)
62. Inspirational Lights: Post-modern*
63. Insp. Lights: Colloquial*
64. Insp. Lights: Classic*
65. Insp. Lights: Erotic*
66.
67.
68.
69.

*Manufactured by LETTERS bookstore.

CATALOGUE ITEM #61

JARRY
BRAND

For those nights
you can't
remember

PLASTER de PARIS

NOW
people will believe that you, like Alfred Jarry, live in the low-ceilinged room of your choice when they see the dust of ceilings atop your duff.

CRITICAL FRAME OF REFERENCE— CATALOGUE ITEM # 22 (PS 37)

INSTRUCTIONS

1) Read instructions thoroughly.
2) Remove F.R.A.M.E.* from envelope.
3) Place F.R.A.M.E. over relevant area of text.
4) Show to doubting friend.
5) Win arguments.

*F(ixed) R(eference) A(nd) M(eaning) E(xplainer)

YES it's *that* easy. Haven't you always hated it when some smart-ass friend, with a few more books under his intellectual belt than you, asks (in that supercilious and absolutely loaded tone), "yes, but what's your critical frame of reference?" Now you can show him and a doubting world too with your very own CRITICAL FRAME OF REFERENCE. Our frame was designed along time-tested lines utilizing the wisdom of the ages as it manifests itself linguistically in the old saw "one picture is worth a thousand words." And how much truer that saying is when the picture is *of* words.

But challenging your friends is just the beginning of what you can do with your very own CRITICAL FRAME OF REFERENCE. Once you start winning arguments there'll be no stopping you.

Now many users have asked us why we call it a "frame" when, in fact, it seems much more like a window. Well that's one of the revelatory features of our patented device. It shows you that any frame of reference is just a window on the world. That's right. And you'll reach new levels of philosophical *and* philological awareness and implication thru the daily application of our device. But wait! There's even more.

With the "Pataphysical Hardware Company's CRITICAL FRAME OF REFERENCE, tho the edges are, in fact, tightly defined, at a distance they blur and become invisible. Thus your critical definitions will appear to cover a much broader area than they actually do— a distinct advantage when dealing with hostile colleagues. Cheaper frames (from less reputable companies) use the now obsolete black border whose funereal aspect properly announces the intellectual death of its users.

I could go on but instead I urge you to take our your frame and begin a thrilling voyage of discovery this very moment. And remember, "at the proper distance the whole world fits inside the frame."

from "S,A's" by A. Gold & N. Guppy
forthcoming from Pata Press

The Poet Disappears into Language and Draws the Door Shut Behind Him
(March 20/80)

W RD

Probable Systems 52:
Some Additional Notes on PS 22 & TTA 25/PS 22a

(November 24/76 thru September 1/86)

There was once a country in which each new thought was seen as demanding a new sign. There were certainly old thoughts, and comfortable well used letters to express those thoughts, but on those occasions when a new thought was formulated it was always accompanied by the formulation of a new-sign.[1]

The paragraph quoted above was the opening paragraph in an unpublished story found among the papers of Carlos Vasquez at his death recently in Toronto. It goes a long way towards providing a theoretical underpinning for the admittedly arcane notions expressed in the rationale behind the translation system first presented in PS 22 (in *Art Facts*). I include it here as an epigram but do not really intend to comment on it any further.

PS 22 is not without problems. To recap briefly: if we consider a text as being written in base alphabet (see PS 11, in *Zygal*), and each word in it as being the complex expression of a single letter, then, by extension, we could look upon the entirety of any text as being simply the complex expression of a single letter. A possible approach was outlined in PS 22 and in TTA 25/PS 22a (in *Art Facts*), another approach was outlined. But both approaches had problems. Primary among these was the question of the title and whether or not it should be seen as expressing the actual base the text is written in or, rather, included as part of the total effect and, hence, the total the translation of the text arrives at. I chose in both of the earlier translations to leave the title out of my calculations entirely. Adding it in made for a much more ludicrous solution, generating, as it did, a letter 4,642,441,660,370,113 letters beyond A. The idea that a mere two words could have been intended to so alter the letter pointed to struck me then, & still strikes me, as fundamentally wrong. But I include it here in these notes in the interests of accuracy and fair play.[2] I leave it to some of my more fanciful colleagues to build their straw houses upon it.

Obviously then I am not simply considering. I am assuming that it is most logical to think of any poem, and indeed any text (genre being a totally superfluous notion in terms of this translation system), to be in base alphabet. In the case of TTA 25, I had the advantage, as the author, of knowing I had written the poem in that base, but what justification is there for thinking any other traditional poem was handled differently. None.

NOTES

1. The story goes on: "Finally there were so many signs that tho one spent a lifetime one could not learn them all. & tho disciples faithfully wrote down new signs as they occurred, they were no longer sure if they were truly new since all that could no longer be known, & even unfamiliar truth dazzled because it seemed new."
2. Tho the argument for using the title as a base indicator is interesting, let us examine in more detail, then, why I think it is ludicrous:

a) We have no examples extant of words where a range of letters greater than those in the base alphabet occupy any of the places. It is certainly conceivable that the signifiers necessary occur in Chinese, Cyrillic &/or other alphabets, that what we are dealing with in most western languages is a limited subset of signs. But then what is the larger subset? And what is the range within which the signs we are using fall? You can see that such questions lead us nowhere.
b) As mentioned above, in "Translating Apollinaire" reading the title as the base (& converting to base ten numerology for easy reference) yields a base of 4,587,655,449,678,542 which means 4,587,655,449,678,515 additional letters are needed to signify the full potential linguistic range of the poem.[3] This seems totally out of line to me. Nonetheless there are translative assumptions here to be settled. Logical outgrowths of the settling of these translative assumptions would be measuring the difference between a title and its text (see PS 28), and measuring the difference between the French and English versions of a poem (see PS 29: A Canadian Concern).
3. On the other hand, it is certainly true that if the poem is in base 4,587,655,449,678,542, then "Translating Apollinaire" in sum is, literally, a single letter/sign 54,786,210,294,570 letters/signs beyond A. The content of the poem would need an additional 4,532,869,239,383,945 letters/signs before the poem moved over into the equivalent of the 10's column. But one of the problems here is that the base was arrived at (as was the text) by translating the words into base ten & adding their values together. What if the space between the words is simply the empty place[4] & the real value of the title is 42,553,880,048,392,020,332,267,444,839,340? What then of the one word poems of Finlay & Clark, where the title far exceeds the text? It makes the most sense to me to simply assume the same relationship between a title & its text in this translative system as in normal speech: a handy way of keeping track of the text which may or my not bear on its content.

4. In a future TTA & PS we will look at this question in more detail. In such a system the various lines of the text must be looked upon as simply lines to be summed. Cf. the author's "counting the ways" for an interesting take on this idea:

love
love
love
love
love
love
love
love
love
love
love
____
I love

Studies in the Book Machine 11

(December 2/82)

DIRECTIONAL
BIAS
3

Before Closure
(1965/66?)

a closet closes. a close loss seen
becomes a loss enacted. all loss seems active
(closest to the heart). closure means
a loss of becoming
becomes
a closet in ourselves
closing.

Three Pages

For Michael Gibbs

leftside suicide rightside

topedge

ledge

bottomedge

right corner

wrong corner

Phrasing
To the memory of Louis Zukofsky
(January 18/79)

1

clusteredtogether
squeezedtightly
literallycrampedforspace

a human condition

humane or
hu may not

tea

& then again

the quali-
the levi-
the lucidi-

2

mental home
a state

strictly within my

proven   shall
(as if to encompass a shift in thot or tone)

meta-

physical
phorical

– man i did not know &

the beginning of
another story

3

the right hand side
the left hand side
the suicide

looking straight
a head

strictly a quest
shun good or evil?

two or
three lives

"one for yourself &
one more for the road"

4

head
thright

number &
number

brailing at the world

b lined like
a honeycomb

honey come home
com' 'ome
mmm

5

& drum corps

arrives

whistling in the dark
do do
        that's it you've got it

6
   6
      6

(1971)

and an a

For Steve McCaffery

Ad Lib ABCD

Ad Lib: 18 36 60

TRG Report 2: Narrative (part 2)
Two Pages on the Nature of the Reality of Writing
For Dick Higgins

the nature of the reality of writing on two pages

transcends the nature of the reality of writing them

Panache Poem

1
the custom
creates the customer

ritual then as
commodity

you go into hock for
the paraphernalia

paranoia
leads you there

2
"i *need* that"

"i can't *do* without it"

two parts of
the same speech

your verb betrays you

where the stress falls's
the action

manifest

your reactions
add the o
MY GAWD!

3
some total

difficult to balance

this art

accounting for

double entry

systems

4
empire
is where the umpire
assumes he's more important than
the players

they're all on waivers
anyway

there's no home team
anymore

just the ubiquitous scoreboard
& the umpire's blinded calls

the endless diamonds
start to look the same

reign of tiara

5
the rich, you-all,
read your glazed eyeballs for
the duller signs

the bucks you pass
pile up in
the club house

accounting for your tastes

accounting for the repetition
the endless cycles of
final games
towards which
you are drawn

like the simile
they are dreaming of

counting on

the metaphor of capitalism

do you want the church to grow god?

what do you get from it?
a bunch of farming sycophants

sucks on
the third planet from
a sun

everyone shouting
gimmee lord
gimmee

(This text exists only on sheets torn from a steno notepad. It is written in pencil and although the text itself is clear, the title is fuzzy. It looks as if the original title was "Panache Poem," but bp wrote a revision over it, making it difficult to decipher. — I.N.)

Vortext
(Toronto, January 25/79; April 19/84)

1
pre occupation
the mind is
not a
blank

"this material is
unsuitable for a
poem"

stress &
feet ache

HOT DOG
/s

imple really

too damn!

put your toe in

2
no false idles

pumping the psyche
iron will

huge gaps between
centred thots
(others rushing in
— birth
— death
— life
— etc.)

i've had my fill
THEE I SING
baby

3
the branches of the trees
press against the roof

ice weighted
snows
          covers the whole thing

still photos

rusting pipes/a sea made out of bricks/
portions of four cars visible between the buildings/

make of it what you will maker

the ache of reason presses

ink flows

4
no good reason at all

he said

again

above the hum of cars on
davenport

above the splash of water &
the howling

roar

5
sound effects

a

        (my mistake)

that was deliberate
(as in
i think i'll wear
two different coloured socks
"proof" of
my schizophrenia)

6
the finger then as index
(viz: i've got it at
      my finger tips)

or
   the tongue
(i.e: i've got it at
     the tip of
     my tongue)

the mind
(i know it's in here
   somewhere)

searching

7
th
(forcing the ryme
out of sight)

won't get there today
anyway

on the verge of something new &
despair

the safe old ways aren't there
any anymore

8
right at the core

friends die by
their own hand or
a lack of reaching

teach oneself something new (again)

how do you tell them
anyone
          how do you get across
the words
the voice
disappearing into futures you cannot know

9
so that's immortality

a selflessness
a willing to let it go

hate it or love it
shouldn't matter to me

me's involved in
a different show

business

                      there's no
go
      into those reaches

sit back &
watch the snow

enjoy it

flung back
out of this state

meant this poem

Unsigned: A Book of the Unwritten

(November/86)

AN INTRODUCTION

This is not a blank book and should not be construed as such. It is not meant to be written in but rather to be "read," seriously, as an attempt to deal with that which is unsigned and lies, therefore, outside the scope of what is writable. Thru the years, in a series of books, one of the issues I've been exploring is what space on a page means, what it notates.

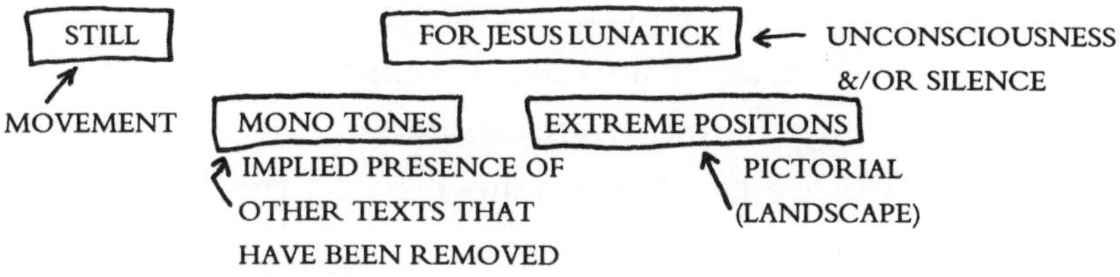

Space is part of what creates meaning. It is not simply absence.

"Unsigned" moves this, conceptually, into a different area: the attempt to point, thru the media what-is-written uses, to that which is unwritable. Unwritable not because of a failure on the part of the writer, but because it lies outside the realm of what is signable. To sign the unsignable, to contain it, in a sense, even tho its containment is at least partially "pataphysical is, nonetheless, to begin, thru paradox, the writing of it in the mind of the reader. The only writing act in this third part is the title and this intro. If "Poetry is the language of an act of attention," the poetry in this case can occur only in the implications of the book structure when considered within the contexts the title "Unsigned," & its various meanings, address.

The first two parts of the book, "Naming 6" and "Naming 7," were written in December 1980. They function as an introduction to some, tho not all, of the issues "Unsigned" attempts to deal with. They provide a kind of frame out of which the reader can move more easily into the implications of the unsigned.

"Unsigned" itself arose out of a footnote to PS 22, and was conceived in November 1986. It is PS 53. Tho the Probable Systems series tends to exist in the realm of the "pataphysical, it also addresses the nature of what is real. I have always loved the experience of someone reading a work of fiction and saying "How true." What follows here is not a fiction at all. It is, in an absolute sense, the truth.

For my great grandparents
Casper and Sarah Leigh,
unknown, unseen
among the many who created me.

I

NAMING 6

object

page

sheet

surface

rectangle

paper

space

thing

II

NAMING 7

word

poem

prose

text

image

sequence

III

UNSIGNED

Additor's Note

"Book was there, it was there. Book was there."
— Gertrude Stein

This was the "pata noster I mumbled to myself while editing this book. With Steinian insistence, & lambent "patalogic, the book certainly was there. The task was to bring it here.

The present volume is the fifth in a series that began with *Love: A Book of Remembrances* (Talonbooks, 1972), *Zygal: A Book of Mysteries & Translations* (Coach House Press, 1985), *Art Facts: A Book of Contexts* (Chax Press, 1990), & *Ox, House, Camel, Door: A Book of Higher Glyphs* (unpublished). The first three books were conceived more closely together than their publication dates would suggest. Around 1972-73, *Zygal* took shape and was recognized by bp as carrying on from where *Love* left off; *Art Facts* "was first conceptualized in the mid-70s."[1] But the series was constipated by the everpending publication of *Zygal.*[2] Barrie's process of amassing material for the books following *Love* was pure accumulation: he'd add a piece to the appropriate file, or files, when it occurred to him that it belonged there. Editing and shaping the book came later. Consequently, there was some overlap of texts among the drafts. Pieces in the *Art Facts* draft were removed because they had been included in *Zygal.* Similarly, several pieces slated for *Truth* had appeared in either *Zygal* or *Art Facts.* So although the "Truth" file in bp's study looked fat & promising, an itemizing of the contents showed it to hold a somewhat thinner, though by no means skimpy, book. Besides previously published pieces, it contained duplicates of texts, texts noted to be included but never located, and detritus. It also held some wonderful writing.

In a letter to Charles Alexander (of Chax Press), which accompanied the final draft of *Art Facts,* bp sketched some of his thoughts on the series. His idea was to

> [continue] certain threads thru this whole series while still allowing each book to stand on its own (it's one of the other notions of the series that each volume should come out from a different publisher). i've also tried to cover a fairly wide formal range (another characteristic of the series). (30 August 1988)

Even a quick riffle thru these pages will reveal an astonishing range of textures: typewriter concrete, hand drawn visuals, found texts, maps, diagrams, lost texts, footnotes, some apparently blank pages, historiographic "pataphyctions, contradictions, theoretical investigations into the secrets of the alphabet and the machinery of the book, a hardware "patalogue, pages identified as such, pages not identified as such, and even some lines that look and read like... poems. There are those serial threads— numbers from

"Kite," "I.T.A.N.U.T.S.," "Sketching," & "Probable Systems," among others. But if these contents seem more diaspora than book, look again. Or, as bp suggested elsewhere, "*read* the book you're *reading*."[3]

While all the books in this series share disparate attentions, each one does indeed "stand on its own," exhibiting its particular research concerns. And the overriding underpinning of *Truth: A Book of Fictions* is "pataphysics.

Rather than give a periphrastic explanation as to the nature of "pataphysics, I offer instead Alfred Jarry's urdefinition:

> Pataphysics, whose etymological spelling should be ἐπι (μετα τα φυσικα) and actual orthography *'pataphysics*, preceded by an apostrophe so as to avoid a simple pun, is the science of that which is superinduced on metaphysics, whether within or beyond the latter's limitations, extending as far beyond metaphysics as the latter extends beyond physics... [P]ataphysics will be, above all, the science of the particular, despite the common opinion that the only science is that of the general. Pataphysics will examine the laws governing exceptions, and will explain the universe supplementary to this one; or, less ambitiously, will describe a universe which can be— and perhaps should be— envisaged in the place of the traditional one, since the laws that are supposed to have been discovered in the traditional universe are also correlations of exceptions, albeit more frequent ones, but in any case accidental data which, reduced to the status of unexceptional exceptions, possess no longer even the virtue of originality.
>
> DEFINITION. *Pataphysics is the science of imaginary solutions, which symbolically attributes the properties of objects, described by their virtuality, to their lineaments.*[4]

Clear enough. But what is Canadian "pataphysics?

> The distinction is subtle: from elision (') to quotation (") through a superinducement on elision ('+' = "). Within the ordinarities of elision the apostrophe places 'pataphysics outside the domain of the Origin... [W]hat then is the status of the elision: (')? The beginnings of 'pataphysics are in that slide (elision) into-beside-beyond the incontrovertible assertion that 'it' or " ' " commence nowhere. Now here (in there) are the parameters (and perhaps we might risk the 'patameters) of a science inscribed within the property of the apostrophe, of the comma inverted and announcing itself as the science of the general inversion and the non-art of the absent.
>
> The Canadian contribution to 'Pataphysics is 'pataphysics' first amendment. To wit, the erasure of "that" elision and the institution of a science of the perpetually open citing. A shift from elision to quotation by way of the doubling of the elide, a doubled inversion and an inverted

doubling. Canadian 'pataphysics gives us then quotation (as Science always is) of the given that we do not understand but with emendations that serve to constitute our explanation... "Pataphysics... will be "the literature of all imaginary sciences."[5]

I made my editorial decisions with "pataphysical delineations in mind, & received further guidance, & reassurance that I was on the right track, from some of bp's notes.

Satisfied that *Art Facts* was on its way to becoming a book, bp could close its forthcoming covers and tend to other projects. In fact, on the day he wrote to Charles Alexander with the final draft, he made two pages of jottings about the next two books in the series, suggesting pieces to be added to both. Facing these notes is a sketch for a cover or title page image for *Truth*: the emblematic " " ". My instinct that *Truth* was to be one of those books partaking in "the never-ending, never-commencing discourse"[6] of "pataphysics was happily confirmed by this finding. A note wondering "what about the "pataphysics catalogue idea?" started my head nodding noisily in affirmation. Some notes about reworking a couple of Probable Systems[7] prompted me to check a disk cataloguing (incompletely) numbers 18-53. There I discovered thirteen of the items in the ""Pataphysical Hardware Catalogue" listed as Probable Systems.[8] Surprisingly, bp inserted only one Probable System (52) in the *Truth* file, but his notes indicate that he was thinking of bringing in others. I believe my additional selections of PS 14, 33, 36, and 53 fall well within the parameters of a "science of the perpetually open citing."[9] Of the five non-hardware Probable Systems, two (52 & 53) are published for the first time. Another series making its debut here is "Studies in the Book Machine." I encountered it in 1989 while I was compiling an inventory of bp's papers after his death. It exists only in notebooks, and nowhere does bp mention it as a probable inclusion in this volume. It seemed to me, however, so obviously integral to the concerns of this book that it *had* to be added.

These lengthy additions to an already sizeable manuscript obliged me to begin a carefully choreographed elimination dance. While maintaining the heterogeneity characteristic of the series, I gave the "pataphysical precedence. I sieved out visuals and short texts that would be better sited in *Ox, House, Camel, Door*— a book attending to the energies of the lettristic image and the eloquence of alphabets. *Truth*, as it "patamorphosed before me, disclosed its prime concerns to be the iconicity of the page, the mechanics of the book, and the fictions of writing & reading. Again and again, the reader is reminded that the page is not a neutral space, a mere holding cell for contents. It is "literally one side of a two-sided sheet of paper— the surface of a three-dimensional object."[10] Confronting this physicality, the reader becomes more aware of her literal involvement with the book machine, with the act of reading. "Unsigned: A Book of the

Unwritten" even asks than the reader be completely responsible for what he is reading.

The numerous synchronicities that occurred during the process of shaping this book made it feel more like a collaborative effort that a solo editing job. Had Barrie put it together himself, it would naturally have been a different book. Such is the fate of all posthumous publications. As it stands, it is "all this and not ordinary, not unordered in not resembling," as St. Ein put it. So, do read the book you are reading, remembering that "the idea of 'truth' is the most imaginary of all solutions."[11]

Irene Niechoda
February, 1993

NOTES

1. Nichol, to Charles Alexander. 30 August 1988.
2. "We promised it to the author in 1973. We promised it to you in 1974 and again in 1980." (Back cover blurb for *Zygal*, 1985.)
3. "When the Time Came." *Line* 1 (Spring 1983): 46-61.
4. "Exploits and Opinions of Doctor Faustroll, Pataphysician: A Neo-scientific Novel" (192-93). Simon Watson Taylor, translator. In *Selected Works of Alfred Jarry*. Roger Shattuck and Simon Watson Taylor, eds. 1965. New York: Grove, 1980. 173-256.
5. "Introduction to *Canadian "Pataphysics"* (301-02). The Toronto Research Group (Nichol & Steve McCaffery) wrote this introduction for a special issue of *Open Letter* (4th ser. 6/7 [Winter 1980-81]), later published by Underwhich Editions as *Canadian "Pataphysics*. I quote from the revised edition of the text as it appears in *Rational Geomancy: The Kids of the Book Machine— The Collected Research Reports of the Toronto Research Group 1973-1982*. Steve McCaffery, ed. Vancouver: Talonbooks, 1992. 301-03.
6. Ibid. 302.
7. These were neither revised, nor included here.
8. **Studies in the Book Machine 8**

   (August 3/82)

   The uselessness of footnotes or the randomness of them, the fiction they create under the text, or aside from, or peripheral to the main body of the speaking.
9. *Rational Geomancy* 301.
10. "The Book as Machine," in *Rational Geomancy* 63.
11. Roger Shattuck, in his "Superliminal Note" to the special issue of the *Evergreen Review* (4.13 [May-June 1960]: 24-33) devoted to 'pataphysics.

Studies in the Book Machine 14
(February 18/83)

if this is a page